CLUES TO THE EXCITEMENT ABOUT
THREE-TIME EDGAR AWARD NOMINEE
ROBERT BARNARD

"He offers a delightful blend of witty social satire and genuine mystery."

—The Washington Post

"Barnard is an amusing Englishman with an eye for the self-delusion and hypocrisy in all of us . . . and the result is a growing series of mysteries that are entertaining, often quite funny . . . and acutely observing."

—The Boston Globe

"There's no one quite like Robert Barnard in his ability to combine chills and chuckles and then sprinkle the whole with delicious irony."

—San Diego Union

"If P. D. James is the heir to Dorothy Sayers, Robert Barnard is fast taking on the Christie/Marsh mantle . . . the most appealing and reliable practitioner of the classic British mystery to arrive here in the last decade."

—Kirkus Reviews

Political
Suicide

Robert Barnard

A DELL BOOK

Published by
Dell Publishing Co., Inc.
1 Dag Hammarskjold Plaza
New York, New York 10017

Dell ® TM 681510, Dell Publishing Co., Inc.

ISBN: 0-440-16946-1

Reprinted by arrangement with Charles Scribner's Sons

Printed in the United States of America

September 1987

10 9 8 7 6 5 4 3 2 1

WFH

Contents

1

Dead Member

It was a quiet Friday morning in Downing Street. The Prime Minister was stewing over a draft bill to privatize the armed forces, many of the aides and secretaries who normally cluttered the place were already off for the weekend, and in the kitchens the cook was preparing a light lunch of staggering ordinariness.

At 10:40 the Prime Minister's Principal Private Secretary tapped on the study door and poked his head in.

"Oh, Prime Minister—just heard on the wires: Jim Partridge is dead."

The Prime Minister looked up from the paper-strewn desk.

"Ask the Chairman when would be the best time for a by-election. I'd have said before the Budget, wouldn't you? And make sure the usual messages are sent— deepest sympathy, and all that."

And the prime-ministerial head bent down over the papers again.

*   *   *

The death of James Partridge, MP for Bootham East, made slightly more stir elsewhere in the country.

"Dead?" said Harold Fawcett, his party agent, warming his backside against the imitation-coal gas fire in his Bootham living-room, and speaking into the telephone on his mantelpiece. "*Dead*, Chairman? But I can't believe it, I saw him—what?—two weeks ago. No, I lie, three. He looked perfectly all right then. He was *what*? Fished out of the Thames? . . . But that's incred . . . Was he *what*? Having an affair? If he was, he wasn't having it in Bootham. Well, he wouldn't be, to be perfectly frank. We're not exactly his type, no disrespect to his memory. And to be honest, I never heard anything like that about him . . . No, *certainly* I never saw him drunk . . . Before the Budget? But is that wise? It will look like a rush job, and it will *be* a rush job . . . Naturally we've no candidate lined up. Partridge was a man of forty-two—we thought he'd be here for decades yet. And if there's going to be flak from his death, I'd have thought it would be *very* unwise to . . . Oh, the PM . . . the PM wants it . . . Right. I'll get on to the Committee at once . . . I'll be back to you, Chairman."

As the day wore on, telephone wires up and down the country began to buzz. Young stockbrokers, gentlemen farmers, bored and ambitious solicitors, research workers at Central Office—all ringing up their friends, their political contacts, each other. Had you heard? Are you interested? What was the majority? The phone at Harold Fawcett's hardly stopped ringing all day: "I say, I've just heard . . . Terrible tragedy, quite appalling . . . at his age . . . Look, old chap, I know it's early days yet, but I was wondering . . ."

So busy was the Bootham Agent's line that when the Party Chairman tried to ring him again from London later in the day, it was forty minutes before he could get through.

"Ah—you've got things well in train? . . . Final selection meeting tentatively set for January 10th. Quite —we've got Christmas intervening, haven't we? Awful nuisance, Christmas" (said the Chairman, a gentleman of impeccable Christian credentials). "Well, if everything goes smoothly then—and I'm sure you'll see that it does—then perhaps we could pencil in, even more tentatively, say Thursday, February 27th, as a pretty good date. That's well before the Budget, and before the Chancellor starts flying kites for the Budget . . . Yes, he is inclined to do that. In fact last time he gave practically the whole thing away in advance . . . Oh yes, and there's one more thing, Harold—I may call you Harold? We'll probably be seeing a fair bit of each other in the near future. Well, I think you should know that the PM will probably want the candidate to be One of Us. Entirely up to you, the choice, of course, but do make it One of Us. Right? I don't have to spell it out, do I? Good! I can see we're going to get on famously."

So what it came down to was that a good seventy per cent of those telephone wires vibrating with life up and down the country represented so much wasted money thrown into the national coffers. All unknowing, the gentlemen farmers, the solicitors in Leeds, the local councillors and the retired army men were basing their hopes on a chimera. They were not One of Us. The more sensible among them, though, were aware of the odds against them, and were far from building castles, or seats, in the air. Those who were One of Us, similarly (young economists of a certain stamp, men in PR, men who'd made their first million by the time they were twenty-five), they knew that the odds were stacked in their favour, and they were chuckling with delight.

"Derek?" said Antony Craybourne-Fisk, on the phone to Derek Manders, the Member for Crawley South, "Have you heard? Jim Partridge has died."

"So I heard," said Manders, surveying the length of an elegantly-trousered leg as he sat in the study of his Mayfair home, bought with a large part of that first million. "But I haven't heard any of the details. What was it?"

"Suicide, so the whisper goes, but I don't think anybody really knows. Dredged up out of the Thames."

"Really? Something of a surprise, isn't it? I hadn't heard any rumours. What was it? Business difficulties?"

"I wouldn't have thought so, would you? Not Jim Partridge. Straight old Jim. Wouldn't have thought it could be sex either, but you never know. It usually is with us. I hope they manage to hush things up—for the good of the by-election. Oh, and on that subject—"

"I thought that might be why you were ringing, Antony. How big was his majority?"

"According to *The Times Guide to the House of Commons*—not that you can trust that—it was close on six thousand."

"Hmmm. Results at the last election were a bit misleading. What was his majority in '79? Something quite small, I fancy. After all, Bootham is hardly natural Tory country, is it? Got any connections in that part of the world?"

"None. Wait a bit though—I think my grandmother was born in Yorkshire."

"Any chance of wheeling her out?"

"I'm not sure. I think she's in a home for decayed Rep actresses in Southsea. For all I know she might be best kept under wraps—senile dementia, or DTs, or something like that. Still, I suppose she could be *mentioned* . . ."

"Quite."

"What I was thinking, Derek, is that you have the ear of the Chairman . . ."

"Oh, I wouldn't say that."

"*And* the PM, if you would but use it. And I thought that if you were to mention my name . . . in passing . . ."

It was not only in the middle and upper echelons of the ruling party that the death of James Partridge was beginning to cause ripples. Ex-Labour MPs—far from an endangered species at the period we are dealing with—were up and down the country ringing each other up: *who* had been the candidate last time, did they know? Was he firmly ensconced there still, or was there a chance for anybody else? "Of course, if *you* were interested, old man, I wouldn't think of sticking my oar in," several of them said, not meaning to be believed, and not being. And at Labour Party Headquarters, two members of the National Executive dis-

cussed the inevitable by-election over two thick cups
of thick tea.

"We've got to put up a good showing there," said
one. "It'll be seen as a test of the new party leader."

"The new leader's had a fair number of tests by now."

"Quite. Some he's come through with flying colours.
Others . . ."

"Exactly. Who's the candidate there?"

"Sam Quimby. He was MP for one of the Manchester seats, you remember. Lost it in '79. Fought
Bootham East in '83—put up quite a good fight. Might
have won it, if it hadn't been for that damned Alliance.
He'll be a good candidate. We'll back him up to the
hilt. Leader, Deputy Leader, Tony Benn, the whole
caboodle. It could be a very promising show, for us."

But unknown to them the matter was in danger of
slipping out of the control of the National Executive
(as so many matters did). At the very moment they
were speaking, a phone call was in progress between
the Hampstead branch secretary of Workers for Revolutionary Action and that movement's Deputy Chair-
person in Deptford. Both were members of the Labour
Party of some three years' standing.

"Have you heard, Sid? Jim Partridge's chucked himself off some bridge or other."

"Who's he when he's at home?"

"MP for Bootham East. Right? Get me?"

"Get you, Frank. Interesting. We've put in a fair bit
of work there, I know. Who's the candidate?"

"Sam Quimby."

"Sam Quimby! He's practically a Tory!" said Sid,
in a voice of practised and patently theatrical outrage

that was not meant to be taken seriously. Sam Quimby was a mildly distinguished ex-MP of impeccably anti-nuclear, anti-American and anti-Common Market credentials.

"Exactly. A point we shall be making as forcibly as we know how over the next few weeks." Frank chuckled happily. "Old Sam's a gentleman, you know. He'll splutter, but he'll go without a fight. *And* put out a statement of support for our candidate. Getting rid of him will be a piece of cake."

"And we're strong there?"

"Couldn't be stronger. Our men and their supporters virtually took over the party a couple of months ago. Sam would have been out on his little pink ear by spring in any case."

"And who'll be the new Labour candidate, then?"

"Well, I'll tell you who we've got in mind. Jerry Snaithe."

"The GLC man?"

"The very one. Chairman of the Arts and Leisure Activities Committee of the Greater London Council. Had lots of publicity over some of his handouts. And rock-solid from our point of view."

"Bootham's in Lancashire, though."

"Yorkshire."

"Same difference. Will they want a Londoner foisted on them? They tend to resent that kind of thing."

"Ah—BUT! Trump Card! Our Jerry just happened to go to school in Yorkshire."

"I didn't know that. That alters things. Where?"

"Amplehurst, actually."

"Isn't that a public school? RC or something?"

"Right. Jerry's dad was a diplomat, and a Holy Roman to boot."

"Well, our Jerry's certainly lived that down, hasn't he?"

"Hasn't he just! And of course all we say in the election address is 'went to school in Yorkshire.' Or even 'grew up in Yorkshire.' The Tory gutter press never dug it up for the GLC elections, so there's no reason why they should now."

"I'd say it was beginning to look promising."

"I'd say it was looking very promising indeed."

"Would he win the seat, do you think?"

"Oh—winning. I don't know about that. But that's not really the point, is it?"

The leader of the Social Democratic wing of the Alliance was talking to the leader of the Liberal wing of the Alliance, during a regular Friday date that was aimed at keeping the Alliance green.

"They're pushing ahead with the by-election at Bootham, you notice."

"So I gather. One of yours at the last election."

"At this one, too."

"Oh, of course. We wouldn't think of interfering. Got anything in mind?"

"Well, there's a perfectly respectable candidate left over from last time, I believe. I campaigned for him, but I can't remember much about him. Local man—councillor, social worker, or teacher, or something. Very worthy. Question is, should we try and draft in one of our senior people. One of our ex-MPs, perhaps."

"Plenty of those."

"You don't have to tell me. What I'd like to know is: would it do more harm than good? In these Northern constituencies it's often the really local man who goes down best. Westminster's another country to them. Then there's the question of whether one of the candidates at least shouldn't be a woman. The Tories won't pick one, they never do, and Labour's got Sam Quimby from the last election. It makes Parliament look like a male club."

"Which it is. Were you thinking of Shirley?"

"I don't know that she wants to get back in yet. Thinks she's beginning to look like a political yo-yo. But there are others. The main thing is, not to give the appearance of dithering."

"Quite."

"Take a decision, and stick to it."

"Exactly."

"I wish I had a clearer picture of what grass-roots opinion in the constituency is likely to be . . ."

And so, determined to give an appearance of not dithering, they dithered.

The day had waned, and the watery half-light of a December dusk had given way to a chill and rainy darkness. The democratic processes which were to determine what choice was to be presented to the electors of Bootham were now so well under way that no one any longer bothered to mention the name of James Partridge, or to pretend that it was much too early to think about the by-election. The Prime Minister had long ago forgotten the death of this back-bencher, and was giving an evening reception for a trade delegation from an obscure and unsavoury Sultanate in the Persian Gulf. But half a mile from Downing Street, in the shabby anonymity of the concrete and glass tower that is New Scotland Yard, Jim Partridge was still a live issue.

"Accident is a physical impossibility," said Chief Superintendent Sutcliffe, stirring a cup of coffee and looking thoughtfully at Inspector Wendell, an old friend, and his own generation of CID man. "He was five foot eight, and the parapet on Vauxhall Bridge would be well above his waistline. He'd have had to be sitting on it to fall off accidentally, and the doc says he definitely wasn't drunk."

He sat there, still stirring, forgetting to drink. He was fifty-seven, and ten weeks off his retirement date: he had a sad, grey moustache and kindly, tired eyes. His wife was dead, his two daughters grown up and married. He looked forward to his retirement with a strange mixture of hope and dread—would it be a liberation, or a death?

"We shan't get a proper post mortem report till tomorrow," he said, "but on the face of it the obvious conclusion has to be that it was suicide."

"Is there any reason why it shouldn't be?"

Sutcliffe shrugged, an uneasy shrug.

"None why it shouldn't, and none why it should, so far. I've only spoken briefly to the wife on the phone, but she said she knew of none. Perhaps she would say that. All they can suggest over at Conservative Headquarters is that he was over-conscientious, and that he's been snowed under with work connected with some private member's bill he was piloting through the House. It doesn't seem much of a reason for suicide."

"I believe they *are* a hell of a lot of work, when you haven't got the government machine behind you."

"Granted. But you don't have to take on a private member's bill if you don't want to. I'll just have to dig a bit deeper if I'm to come up with something that will satisfy the inquest."

"Careful. It could be a hot potato. Keep the Old Man informed."

"Oh, I will, naturally. Powerful Interests, as they call them, will be having their say. One thing about a political thing like this: I'll have to get it right, or I'll certainly be shot at from one side or the other. On the other hand, the worst thing you can do with something political is to try and sweep all the dirt under the carpet."

He was quite wrong, of course. Before long it was being made clear to him from all sides that the one thing they wished more than any other was that he had swept all the dirt under the carpet. But by then it was too late.

2

Private Member

Penelope Partridge was tall and elegant—no trace of disarray on this her second morning of widowhood. Her face was long and handsome, and all suggestion of the horse was kept at bay by skilful make-up. The eyes were dry but slightly reddened, almost (thought Sutcliffe, but kicking himself at the same time for the inbred cynicism of policemen) as if she had deliberately rubbed them before his visit, but not too much. Was she a good MP's wife? he wondered. He couldn't see her going down well in Bootham— not with that cool, reserved, condescending manner. Already he was being given the idea that being interviewed by a policeman, whatever his rank and whatever the circumstances, was something very much beneath her dignity. She was trying to make him feel like an upper servant.

"Of course, looking *back*," she was saying, with an upper-class drawl that emphasized unlikely words, "one can see that his problem was that he was too conscientious—he let things prey on him, took them too much to heart."

"Personal things, you mean?"

Sutcliffe was surprised to see a flicker of apprehension flash through her eyes, but it was not allowed to change the expression on her face, and she retrieved herself immediately.

"Oh no—*no-o-o*," She glanced around the drawing-room of their elegant Chelsea house, as if to say: who, having this, could have personal problems? "I meant political problems, of course. Governmental problems. He was a junior health minister, you know, for three years—dropped in the reshuffle after the last election. Dropped, just like that." A trace of bitterness invaded her tone, but again she shook it off immediately. "I have a feeling the PM likes people who can take things a bit more in their *stride*; don't go around with the burdens of the world on their *shoulders* the whole time. That was James's problem: he worried, couldn't leave a thing alone if it was on his mind. I remember when he was having some troubles in the Department—you know, nurses' pay and suchlike—" she waved a long-fingernailed hand—"and he went to open some hospital or other, and there was a big demonstration—you know the kind of show they put on. They heckled him, and threw things—quite nasty, but of course if you're a minister *these* days, with current standards of behaviour, you have to get used to that sort of thing. But you know, for a week afterwards he could talk about nothing else—their case, pay guidelines, violence—until I could have screamed! Really, in politics these days one has got to be a bit more—

insouciant. Happy-go-lucky," she added, for Sutcliffe's benefit.

"I see. So you think that that was why his career never really . . . took off?"

"I'm sure of it. He never got his priorities right—never worked out even what they were. I used to say to him, either you go all out for office, high office—because otherwise all this Westminster stuff is sheer drudgery, and damned dull to boot—or else you go after money. Let's face it, James wasn't born to money: he set up this small printing and duplicating business when he was quite young, with some money he was left. It was very efficient, used very modern methods and so on, and it positively spawned other little businesses all over the country. But James lost interest. Sold out. You've got to be single-minded if you want to make a *lot* of money."

"Instead he went into politics?"

"Exactly. And he always kept very busy, even as a back-bencher. But he was much too wet—politically wet, I mean—to get anywhere much. And there doesn't seem to be any point unless you *do*, not in my book."

"Perhaps not," murmured Sutcliffe. "Was there any political problem in the last few weeks that seemed to be bothering him?"

"Well—" she seemed uncertain—"nothing special that I can *recall.* Constituency problems, naturally. He was depressed by the rising unemployment in Bootham. Have you been to Bootham, ever? No, well it's not the sort of place one *goes* to, deliberately. Between you and me, a *frightful* hole. He found the problems of the unemployed families terribly depressing, though one does sometimes feel, doesn't one, that *some* of them

have almost brought it on them*selves*, and if you can't
do anything about it, there's not much point in bringing
all their problems home. But there—that was James."

"So you didn't live in the constituency?"

"Good Lord, no. Well, we have a cottage. In a little
village called Moreton. Very much *outside*: still in the
constituency, but not *in* Bootham. Bootham East is the
better part of town, naturally, but even so there wasn't
anywhere where I'd care to *live*, even for the odd weekend. We used the cottage when we went up on constituency business—James for his fortnightly surgery,
me to open something or other. I'll get rid of it now,
of course. Though, really—house prices in Yorkshire
are rock *bottom*."

"Tell me: Thursday night, when he didn't come
home—weren't you worried?"

"Well, I didn't *know*. I can see I shall have to en-
lighten you, Superintendent, as to how politicians' wives
live, what they have to put *up* with."

"You mean the hours—all-night sittings, and so on?"

"Exactly. And when they don't sit late, all the ma-
nœuvrings and conspirings, and the constituency business, and Christ knows what. We—we have a guest
bedroom here, of course, and we have an agreement
that if James comes in—came in—after I'd gone to bed,
then he slept there. So really, when I didn't see him all
day, I wasn't in the least surprised, because that was
very much business as usual. I went to bed at—oh,
about half past eleven, I suppose, and never gave a
second thought to James's not being home."

"And when you found out in the morning that he
hadn't slept in the spare bed?"

"Well, actually, I didn't. I mean, I came down to

get the children's breakfast—I do that once or twice a week, because we've got a Danish *au pair*, and she gives them the oddest things on rye bread, so I do try to make sure they have something sensible now and again. And I was just sitting down to my own when your sergeant came."

"And then you went up and found the bed hadn't been slept in, I suppose."

"Naturally, of course it hadn't. I understand the body had probably been in the water some hours."

"That's what we think. I'll be getting the results of the post mortem later today. So you can't think of any special reason—?"

But they were interrupted by the entrance of two wide-eyed children, very neat and clean, and an enormous flaxen-haired girl who looked as if she was about to play Brynhild in some open-air Scandinavian pageant play. Sutcliffe knew all too well the sort of questions intelligent five- and six-year-olds ask when they have just lost a parent. Muttering that he would get in touch, and that he hoped Penelope Partridge would contact him if she thought of anything relevant, he made a discreet exit. Walking from the front door to his car, he thought what a very unsatisfactory interview this had been, without being able quite to pin down in his own mind the reasons for his dissatisfaction. But one thing was certain: Mrs Partridge had not been able to put on even a pantomime of sorrow or regret.

The press-cuttings on James Partridge which Sutcliffe found waiting for him in a folder on his desk at New Scotland Yard confirmed the picture that his wife had

painted so pitilessly—that of a man whose career had
never quite got off the ground. Early on in his stint as
a junior minister a newspaper had called him "the thinking man's Tory," and the label had stuck, possibly
because there was so little competition. The occasion
for the label had been a thoughtful speech on the nature
of conservatism which could, by a generous stretching
of the term, have been called philosophical. He had
made one or two more such speeches, and it was perhaps to give him more time to think his conservative
thoughts that the Prime Minister had dropped him from
the government after the election. He had apparently
accepted his dismissal without bitterness, had only joined
one revolt against the government since, and seemed
determined to be a conscientious back-bencher and a
good constituency MP. He had appeared three years
before in the "New Boys" column in the scandal sheet
Private Eye, but they had found little dirt to fling at
him. He had busied himself in recent months with a
Private Member's Bill which one of the papers had
dubbed "The Animals' Charter."

Sutcliffe digested all this, and then he got on the
phone to Conservative Central Office. The girl on the
switchboard said that of course it *was* a Saturday, and
there was only the tiniest skeleton staff there, just to
deal with any emergency that came up, and naturally
the Chairman wasn't there, but he could come and talk
to Terry if he wanted to. Who was Terry? Well, Terry
was sort of deputy-under-constituency-organizer—she'd
forgotten his exact title, but he was a sort of liaison
man. Sutcliffe said he'd come and talk to Terry.

Terry, it turned out, was just out of university, well-

groomed but amiable, with a shapely haircut of medium
length that failed to hide the fact that he was wet behind
the ears. Yes, actually he had known Jim Partridge,
not just since he took up this job, but—well, his father
was in the House, actually ("On the government side?"
asked Sutcliffe innocently), and he'd got to know a lot
of the members, well—ever since he was a kid, actually.
And then he'd had a bit to do with Partridge more
recently, actually over this Animals' Charter as the papers were calling it, so really you could say that he'd
known him quite well. Actually.

"And what sort of man was he?"

"Quiet, conscientious, a bit of a plodder. The sort
Ted Heath used to like. Give him a job, and you knew
he'd do it, and well, though he might take quite a lot
of time over it. A good enough speaker, slightly dull
—but actually this isn't the golden age of political oratory, is it? They used to call Michael Foot one of the
great speakers, so the standard *must* be low. If you
were really prepared to listen, Jim's speeches were worth
the effort."

"You never heard of any personal problems?"

"No. But I wasn't on those terms. I'm frightfully
junior here, actually. We came into contact over this
animals bill, and that was giving him problems enough,
heaven knows."

"You think that might have been the reason—?"

"Oh, I didn't say that. Jim was a professional politician, and he'd probably learned to take that sort of
thing in his stride."

"What sort of thing, exactly? What were the problems that the bill was giving him?"

"Well, you might say it was a bill designed in one way or another to offend the maximum number of people. Actually, if you want to know, it was my job to try and warn him off. There was nothing in it for us—as a party, I mean—and there were pitfalls every inch of the way. It was a very comprehensive bill, designed to protect domestic and wild animals against all sorts of cruelty and exploitation. If you want to know who it offended, I could just name, for starters: the hunting and shooting lobby; research scientists; farmers —particularly the intensive kind; furriers; the cosmetics industry—well, you name it, they disliked it, except for the ecology lobby."

"It seems odd I haven't heard more about it."

"It's still in its early stages. But all the specialist journals of these various pressure groups got whiff of it long ago, and they were beginning to alert their people and emit squawks of outrage. I tell you, as far as his career was concerned, it was political suicide . . . Oh, I say, rather an unfortunate phrase, actually, eh?"

"But surely there was nothing much there to offend the electors of Bootham?"

"I don't know about that: dearer food, steep increase in dog licences . . . But I wasn't thinking of that, I meant only that he could say goodbye to any thought of getting high office."

"Since he'd been dropped, there wasn't much thought of that anyway, was there?"

"Well, I suppose, looking around at all the people who have been dropped, no—not very much. They tend to stay dropped. Most of them start giving more and more of their time to the City—directorships in big companies, and so on. Jim took up animals. Really, it was *awfully* un-Conservative."

"Conservation isn't a Conservative thing, then?"

"Hardly. Game conservation, of course, but that's in order to shoot them afterwards."

"Can we come back to the unpopularity of this bill? You implied there'd been squawks in the *Chicken Farmers' Gazette*, or whatever. Had the opposition taken any other form? Threats?"

"That sounds awfully melodramatic. If an MP gets a threat, he generally takes it up with the Speaker as a matter of privilege. But anyone in the public eye receives an amount of hate-mail, you know. Almost all from nuts, and usually pretty mad and full of violence. I'd have thought the pro-animal lobby usually had a fair number of those people in their ranks: there's nothing more violent than the Annual General Meeting of the RSPCA. I think that if Jim received any mail of this sort it was less the manic type, more from the sort of people who felt their livelihood was being threatened."

"You don't know of any specific threats?"

"No. Jim talked generally about 'pretty nasty letters,' but he didn't give any details. You'd have to go along and ask Arthur Tidmarsh—he might know more."

"Who's he?"

"The Labour MP who was sponsoring the bill with him. It was a sort of cross-bench effort—probably more support on their side than on ours, if the truth be known, though the Leadership was wary there too: dearer food isn't popular with anyone except battery hens. If there were any threats—that was what you had in mind?—"

"Yes."

"Then I'd guess he would know more about it than I would, since perforce they'd got pretty close . . . I say, this *was* a suicide, wasn't it?"

"That's for the jury at the inquest to decide," said Sutcliffe, in classic phrase.

"No, but I say, I mean—the inquest will decide pretty much as you tell them to, won't it?" The schoolboy face had gone quite red with consternation. "This business is causing embarrassment all round, you know. I can tell you, we weren't pleased you had to rule out accident. The PM was pretty shirty, because suicide doesn't make the best impression, does it? I mean 'the Almighty hath fixed his canon against self-slaughter,' or however it goes."

"Is it God, or the Prime Minister you're more worried about?" asked Sutcliffe, and murmuring his thanks for assistance he escaped out into Smith Square.

Arthur Tidmarsh proved gratifyingly easy to contact. He was MP for a South London constituency, and lived on the spot in a semi whose living-room was given over entirely to his constituency work: piles of letters, reports, forms and applications, blue books and newspapers. Arthur Tidmarsh seemed at home in the room—more so, in fact, than with his resentful-looking wife and family.

"He was a good bloke in his way," he said, settling Sutcliffe down in an armchair and taking a seat himself at his desk. "Stiffish, reserved, but once you got to know him, tremendously fair. And conscientious to a fault."

"You did get to know him?"

"Oh yes. On a business level, a political level."

"But he didn't, for instance, tell you anything about problems in his private life?"

"Oh no—never anything like that. Not even when we were having a drink together in the bar. We never got within miles of the personal. Was he having problems?"

"That's what I'd like to know."

"All politicians have problems with their private lives: they either have too little of it, or too much. Some dance on the tightrope all their lives—like Lloyd George—and never fall off; and others ruin their career the first time they step off the strait and narrow. It's all bloody unfair, but I suppose you just have to have a flair for it."

"A flair for adultery? It's an idea. Would you say Jim Partridge had it?"

"Well, frankly, no. Jim was more like one of us than a Tory, in some ways. If he'd had an affair, he'd have agonized about it in his conscience. All a Tory cares about is not getting caught."

"About this bill—you're having a bit of hate-mail, I gather."

"Some. It's early days yet. As far as I'm concerned, it wouldn't be worth it if we weren't." He grinned with what was meant to be engaging candour, though Sutcliffe recognized it as a "we're all crooks underneath" smile, such as he had received from innumerable hardened cases. "I'm in it for the publicity as much as anything."

"Was there anything particularly vicious in any of the letters?"

"Not that I recall. Fairly standard stuff, in point of

fact. 'You care more about animals than humans'—that kind of thing. Odd argument that, isn't it? They're not alternatives at all, but people keep wheeling it out. I'd be less worried about the nuts—because not one in ten thousand is actually going to do anything about it—than about the people with special interests: the intensive farmers, the cosmetics industry, the mink farmers: they'd be the ones most likely to act. Though I can't see them doing so in this case."

"Why not?"

Again there was that grin, intended to express engaging honesty. Probably Tidmarsh had built his career on that grin.

"Because it hadn't a chance. Can you imagine a House with a large Tory majority passing a bill that restricts fox-hunting, abolishes stag-hunting, controls game shooting, sets up standards for factory farming more stringent than anywhere else in the world has—and so on, and so on. The only possible way it could get on the statute book would be for us to drop or water down the provisions, one after another, and get left at the end with a totally toothless bill. It's what *will* happen, now he's gone. If I don't decide to drop it altogether. Partridge was a good manager—he'd have been very good in the Whips' Office. I don't fancy all the drudgery now he's gone."

"Going back a moment, do you remember if there was any one of these letters from the various special interest groups that particularly upset him?"

"Well, of course, if he worried about any, he'd worry about ones from his own constituency. We all would. After all, we have to go back and ask the buggers for their votes every four or five years. Jim had one pretty

unpleasant one from a battery farmer in his constituency—abusive, said he could whistle for his vote in
the future."

"A farmer? In his constituency?"

"That's right. It takes in a bit of rural land to the
east of the town. Otherwise I doubt Bootham would
ever have had a Tory MP at all . . . That's the only one
I can remember affecting him. And I don't think it was
the threat, such as it was. He said he'd seen that farm,
seen those hens . . . And you know, we all get that
sort of letter from time to time. We get our own little
formulas for writing back. No doubt Jim had his, and
I expect he forgot it in a day or two."

"It certainly doesn't seem much of a motive for suicide."

"No. Beyond the fact that Jim was decidedly a wor-
rier, in his quiet, ingrowing way. And of course, to
use a cliché, things can pile up. I see it all the time in
my constituency work: you're unemployed, your wife
has left you, but it's the big electricity bill through the
letter-box that's the last straw."

"Maybe," said Sutcliffe, getting up to take his leave.
"But that's not the kind of thing that's easy to put to
an inquest jury."

Driving back to New Scotland Yard, Sutcliffe tried
to sort out the various uneasinesses he had felt during
his day of interviews. In the end, he whittled them
down to two questions: if Jim Partridge was currently
worried over his Animal Protection Bill, why had it
never once been mentioned by Penelope Partridge? And
hadn't she accepted rather too readily his failure to
return on Thursday night? Sutcliffe hadn't a very detailed knowledge of House of Commons procedures,

but he had a vague notion that by Thursday things at the Palace of Westminster were often beginning to wind down, so that members could if possible have a long weekend with their families, or go off to their constituency. As soon as he got back to his office he got on the phone to Arthur Tidmarsh.

"Sorry to bother you again, but did you in fact have business with Partridge on Thursday?"

"Yes, I saw him briefly in the afternoon. Just a little technicality of phrasing. We talked for ten minutes, no more."

"The bill wasn't coming before the House next day?"

"Not this week, no. Yesterday there was just the Coastline Protection Bill, which is a great yawn."

"The House didn't sit late on Thursday?"

"No, it didn't. It was what we call a Dead Thursday."

"Dead Thursday?"

"The government gets all the week's business over early, so we can all get off. Not more than a handful would be in Westminster for the Coastline Protection Bill."

"I see."

"Matter of fact, we hardly ever sit late these days. To the best of my recollection the House rose about eight on Thursday."

"Thank you. Thank you very much."

It was all vaguely intriguing. But when Sutcliffe looked down at his desk, putting down the phone, he found the report of the post mortem, as well as reports from various men on the beat who had been drafted on to the case. Sutcliffe stewed for some time over the post mortem. The pathologist was clearly not entirely happy.

Deceased had drowned, and the body contained only a small amount of alcohol. He had apparently eaten lunch and afternoon tea, the latter a few hours before he died. There were bruises on the body that *could* be consonant with violence having been used, but there was nothing that could *not* have been caused by his hitting a boat, or the pillars of the bridge, when he first fell into the river. All in all, the pathologist had found nothing specific on which to pin his unease. One of the detective-constables had reported that a night watchman in one of the large office blocks on either side of the Tate Gallery end of the Vauxhall Bridge had reported a loud cry around 10:30 on Thursday night, followed by a splash. He had been out on the embankment wall, having a quiet can of beer, the constable thought. He had peered into the water, seen nothing, then gone back inside.

All in all, there seemed nothing to do but go for an open verdict. But Sutcliffe expressed his unhappiness to the Assistant Deputy Commissioner.

"I'm going to wait," he said. "I've got a feeling in my bones that things are not quite right. And I've also got a feeling that something will turn up."

"Micawber," said the Assistant Deputy Commissioner. "But you're probably right. In politics, something or other usually does turn up."

In this case, it took its time. Christmas, that inconvenient Christmas, intervened, and it was well into January before the little man in Battersea saw the picture in the paper, and came along to see Sutcliffe with his worries.

3

A Process Of Selection

The town of Bootham was situated in
South Yorkshire, not very far from the Nottingham-
shire border, and about as near to Sheffield as anyone
would want to be. Its history stretched back to the
Middle Ages, when it had been an important market
town, but local historians who tried to make their fel-
low-townsmen aware of this medieval heritage gave every
appearance of making bricks without straw, for the
Bootham of today was essentially the creation of the
Industrial Revolution, and that demanding, devouring
movement had swept away all trace of earlier, quieter
times. Bootham's nineteenth-century prosperity was
built on steel, and on the coal seams nearby, on the
manufacturing industries which sprang up in the form
of innumerable small factories and workshops. "Where
there's muck there's brass," said the Victorians, convinced they were uttering an eternal verity.

Nowadays, where there was muck, there was just
muck. The prospect seen from the train of decaying

suburbs, disused factories, worked-out mines was only
an extreme statement of what was to be seen everywhere
in the town. As work had become rare, the whole physical structure of the town seemed to have collapsed,
and the whole social structure with it. Though the den-
izens of the South were convinced that the unemployed
were living off the fat of the land, in Bootham one saw
shoddily clad women wheeling dirty babies in decrepit
prams, men standing idly round on street corners, and
a general air of a working people coming to terms with
a future of idleness, of a hearty people wondering where
their next french fry sandwich was coming from. In the
commercial centre, small shops were boarded up, slogans disfigured the walls and litter lined the streets, and
the air was thick with the smells of cheap take-away
foods.

There were, to be sure, parts of Bootham less over-
poweringly dismal. The town was not large, and around
it stretched long fields of barley and of rape, which last
crop in the spring made a display of bilious brilliance
which relieved the eye after all the greys and browns.
In James Partridge's old constituency, Bootham East,
there were still some substantial Victorian houses with
jungles of heavy green shrubs around them, and more
modern detached and semi-detached houses which be-
spoke a certain prosperity—or an ability to command
a fairly considerable mortgage. Here were Tory voters
—but how firm was their commitment, as they sensed
the tide of decay rising towards their feet? This was a
question all the party agents asked themselves, as December shaded into January.

That view from the train was seen by Antony Craybourne-Fisk as the train neared Bootham on January 9th. Christ, what a dump! What am I doing here? were Antony's irrepressible thoughts, though as he saw the platform begin to slide slowly by, he set his face into an expression of unquenchable optimism. He need not have troubled. He was not being met, and nor were the three other hopeful candidates who, unknown to him, were on the same train. Central Office had made it clear that he should be treated no differently from any other potential candidate, except in one small respect; they would prefer it if he were chosen. Antony marched down the platform, over the bridge, registering with his trained candidate's eye that the station gave every appearance of being one that British Rail was intending to close down ("possible future campaign issue"), and then commandeered the one waiting taxi outside the entrance.

Antony had booked into the best hotel in town, which turned out to be not a glass and concrete monstrosity, part of a chain, but a Victorian monstrosity whose owners had tried desperately hard to be bought out by a chain, to be met only by superior smiles and shakes of the head. Everything about Antony's room at the Unicorn was large, there was that to be said for it, but what use is a large bath with no plug? Lunch in the dining-room was large too—a collection of the most appalling and over-cooked mush. Antony was sorely tempted to do what he normally would have done in such circumstances—fuss, fume, shout, abuse—but he told himself that among the slovens and incompetents who ran the place there must be possible future constituents, so he contented himself with saying, as he went past Reception on his way to prospect around the town:

"Could you make sure there's a plug for my bath by the time I get back?"

The man behind the desk, cigarette in mouth, barely looked up from the racing page he was studying.

"They don't make plugs for them baths any more. But I'll see what I can do, mate."

Gulping down one more spurt of rage, Antony Craybourne-Fisk passed through the swing doors of the Unicorn Hotel and out into the street. In the first five minutes of his prowl around the town that he intended should be the springboard of his brilliant career, Antony found that he loathed the place. Bootham was a town of some eighty thousand souls, but bodies were what you noticed first: the broad, heavy, assertive men; the broad, heavy assertive women; the beer guts, the pub-brawl biceps, the pendulous breasts, the fat bottoms. Flab, said Craybourne-Fisk self-righteously to himself: Bootham symbolized the British flab that this government was trying to slim away. But on thinking it over, he decided it seemed less than hopeful to represent a constituency that deserved to be slimmed out of existence.

He tried to look around for more hopeful features. In the centre of the town there remained the top halves of some tolerable eighteenth-century houses, but the ground floors were stereo shops, boutiques and car-part dealers which, having eaten the houses' lower extremities, seemed to be pausing before gobbling the top halves too. The Anglican church was a neo-Gothic construction, ponderously uninspired, the work of a Victorian architect who had sold virtually identical designs to Catholics in Bolton and Congregationalists in Bristol. Antony's very legs seemed to grow disheartened, and the drizzle which had begun, mingy but insistent, fell from a sky that seemed no higher than the church spire. Antony looked for the tenth time at his watch. It was not yet three. The pubs would still be open. As soon as he went past one that seemed quiet, he turned and went in.

He had no sooner got to the bar than a juke-box started up, a wailing, mindless shriek, underpinned by a murderous bass. He turned: the only other person in the bar was a skinny, vacant youth in jeans that were more like tights, and a studded leather jacket. He lounged over the juke-box, and stared back at Antony, evilly incurious. Antony sighed and ordered a double scotch.

"Stranger here?" asked the landlord, and then had to shout it again over the din.

"That's right."

"Don't get many strangers here," said the man, obviously thinking it a point in Bootham's favour.

"No . . . Not really a tourist spot, I suppose . . ." Impelled to honesty by the sense of desolation which even he, an insensitive soul, felt, Antony added: "Bootham looks pretty awful in the rain."

"It looks even worse in sunlight," said the barman complacently. "We don't go in for the pretty-pretty in Bootham."

"No," said Antony Craybourne-Fisk, "No-o-o. You couldn't turn that music down, could you?"

"More than me life's worth, mate," said the landlord, nodding towards the skinny youth. Antony downed his whisky and left.

At three-thirty Antony was scheduled to meet

Bootham's Conservative party agent. He bought a street
guide, and found the place without difficulty. He approached the front door with something like furtive-
ness, but he found he needn't have bothered.

"I'm seeing all the would-be candidates," said Harold Fawcett, cheerfully. "This is no special favour. Of
course I know Central Office would be happy if you
were chosen. You're 'One of Us,' as the Chairman puts
it, and in on the party's wavelength at the moment.
But I tell you, it's not yet in the bag."

"Of course not," said Antony deprecatingly. "Naturally not."

"There's seven to be interviewed by the selection
committee tomorrow. Of these, I'd say three were in
with a chance. Four, if you count the lass. We don't
go much on lady members, in Yorkshire. Should be
home, caring for the kids—that's how we see it. Still,
you never know. But your main opponents are local
men."

"You think there might be a feeling for a local man
this time?"

"I'd say—going by my soundings—that they'll be
split down the middle. On the one hand the local man
is closer to the constituency. On the other, the man
from Central Office is more likely to get the ear of the
government—have friends in high places, be able to get
things done. And I won't hide it from you, Bootham
needs something doing for it."

"Yes," said Antony.

"Now, if you'll take a tip from me, young fel-
low—"

"I really would appreciate one," said Antony, with
something approaching sincerity.

"Well, living in Bootham these days can be depressing. Unemployment, bankruptcies, poverty—we've got it all. Not so much in your constituency, mind—but it's easy to say 'I'm all right, Jack,' if you live down South, less easy if Jack lives two or three streets away and his kids are hungry and he's defaulting on his mortgage. You get my meaning?"

"I think so."

"So what the committee will be looking for is a message of hope." Antony's heart sank to his boots. "Just a touch of optimism, a feeling of light at the end of the tunnel. We've been told often enough that it's there, but we never see it, not here in Bootham. What we want is some slogan—zippy, and heart-raising. Some message to make us square our shoulders and put our chins up. You think up something along those lines, and you're made."

"Oh," said Antony, standing up and buttoning his Burberry. "Yes, I see. Well, you've given me plenty to think about. I think I'll go back to my hotel and try and concoct something of the kind you've mentioned. Something—how shall I put it?—uplifting. By the way, is there anywhere tolerable to eat in town?"

"Where are you staying?"

"The Unicorn."

"Well, you couldn't do better than the dining-room at t'Unicorn. They do you proud there."

"Oh—ah—I'm sure you're right. Thank you very much."

Antony was so depressed by the interview, and by the strain of suppressing his naturally bad temper, that on the way back to the hotel, walking through the still-falling drizzle, he actually bought a book, a thriller, to

while away the time before the interview. He read a
chapter before dinner, had a bath by dint of stuffing a
wad of newspaper down the plughole, and then turned
with a groan to the sheaf of papers with facts and figures
about Bootham, made available to him by Central Office. Over dinner (rump steak, fillet steak or sirloin
steak, all served with french fries and the usual trim-
mings), he gazed at the heavy bodies at the other tables,
hunched over their knives and forks as if they were
garden tools, feeding themselves stolidly, regularly, with
lethargic insistence, and he wondered what in God's
name he was doing in this place, and wondered what
conceivable message of hope he could bring to this
constituency beyond redemption.

But Antony, for all his personal awfulness—or perhaps because of it—was a political animal at heart, and
over the fruit salad (with synthetic whipped cream and
a glacé cherry) there came to him from the ether, via a
political mind trained to tune itself in to every local
ethos and ambience, the faint stirrings of an idea, that
almost made him smile to himself. It was only a beginning, but it could be worked on, could be polished.
And it might go down well. It might be what they were
after. Yes. He took from his jacket pocket a little notebook, and scribbled in it.

Thus it was that, next day, after talking bonhomously
with some of the other hopeful candidates, and implying that he, an outsider, clearly had no hope at all of
being chosen, and after talking for five minutes to the
selection committee of some sixteen souls (decidedly
corporeal souls, most of them) and having explained
that no, he was not married, but that he was young—

well (disarming smile), youngish—and he expected to remedy this deficiency in time, thus it was that Antony perked up imperceptibly as he sensed the approach of a line of questioning that seemed likely to provide him with his opportunity.

"Mr—er—Fisk, you're not from this area?"

"No, that's true—though there are—er—family links."

"We're not an attractive part of the country . . . We have our problems, with unemployment, businesses closing, and so on . . . I wonder how you react to—well, to the place as a whole. Coming, as you do, from the South."

In the earlier questioning, Antony had sensed that split in the committee that Harold Fawcett had mentioned; half of them sceptical, half of them for him, because they'd been told he was a bright boy. Now, if ever, was the time to convert the sceptical. Now he had to swing them. He thrust his whole body forward, blazing with sincerity.

"I saw all the things you're talking about. I saw all the closed works, the empty factories. But it didn't depress me. Shall I tell you how I see it? *Industrial decay is industrial opportunity.* Those aren't closed-down factories, they're factories waiting to be opened up. The microchip revolution—"

To give more is unnecessary, though in fact it flowed on for some time. As an argument it was asinine, rather on the level of the politician who demanded that newspapers should print not the numbers of the unemployed, but the numbers of people who actually had jobs. Whatever the microchip revolution did for Brit-

ain, it was unlikely to do it in the disused kitchen utensil
and garden implement factories that once had given
work in Bootham. But the phrase had the right ring.
It breathed hope, it sketched in that elusive light at the
end of the tunnel. At the end, after a series of run-off
votes, Antony beat one of the local men by ten votes
to six. He was the one who would be recommended
to the General Meeting of Bootham's Conservatives.
He modestly expressed great surprise, though he was
obviously "tremendously pleased" as well.

Later on, over beer at the Conservative Club, Harold
Fawcett chatted over the selection meeting with Sir
Richard Rayne, who owned land on the borders of the
constituency, and he expressed surprise at the margin
of Craybourne-Fisk's victory.

"Thought he might get it, but not by so many. Didn't
expect him to get *your* vote. Was it the hopeful side of
his performance?"

"Not at all."

"Did you like the chap better than you expected?"

"I did not. He's a horrible little shit."

"Why did you vote for him then?"

"I've got a feeling in my bones we're going to lose
this by-election, and it's best we lose it with a little shit
sent down by Central Office. Then we can put a local
man in for next time."

Jerry Snaithe did not arrive in Bootham for the Labour
Party selection meeting by train, but by car. Jerry Snaithe
was essentially a loner. He talked a lot about collective
action, collective decisions, and workers' collectives,
but essentially he was a loner, and the car is the loner's

form of transport. He arrived alone. His wife was working, he said, and in any case he didn't believe in turning the process of selection into a beauty parade. Once within the town limits of Bootham, he drove round the town three times, partly because the traffic system, dreamed up by a sadist in the Town Hall, made it almost impossible to do other than drive round in circles, partly because he wanted to get the feel of the place. He sniffed; he sensed the poverty and aimlessness; he saw the decay and dereliction. Like Lancelot Brown confronted by ancestral acres, he saw the place had "capabilities."

After two circuits of the town he had located the Great Northern Commercial Hotel (Temperance), and after three he drove into its parking yard. He registered, chucked his hold-all into his poky room (hardly noticing anything beyond its number), and, taking a sheet of paper from his inside pocket, he went out into the street. He had, he told himself, to "get busy."

By getting busy, Jerry Snaithe did not mean he was going to meet the people of Bootham and talk over their problems. Nor did he mean that he was going to nobble the selection committee in advance to ensure his selection as candidate. It was not necessary. Workers for Revolutionary Action had occupied twelve of the thirty places on the Bootham General Management Committee since the previous summer and had seven sympathizers in their pockets. When, in December, one week after the death of James Partridge, the committee had decided that the re-selection of their previous candidate was not to be automatic, this was only the public expression of a previous *fait accompli*. When Sam

Quimby, the previous candidate, had told the *Bootham Evening Advertiser* that he had always been in favour of re-selection, but that he regretted that the local party in Bootham East had been taken over by a tightly organized cell of Marxist activists, it was tantamount to an admission of defeat. The political correspondents of the national press had said that this decision meant that the seat was "up for grabs," but they were wrong, and Jerry Snaithe had known they were wrong. It was all arranged. He had not come to Bootham for selection, but for coronation.

So when he told himself to "get busy," he did not mean organize his own selection, but to plan with his friends his future campaign. He went to the men on his list, and the woman, to Harry, Sid, Arthur, Fred, Quentin, Percy, Sean and Alice, and they planned strategies, speakers, tactics. In the evening he met the rank and file members of the WRA, all nineteen of them, at Alice's. Alice made some sandwiches, and they all had, as Jerry told her at the end, "a great time." By the end of the day they'd got together a list of potential speakers and campaigners. They'd got Albert Spadgett, a Trade Union leader who vied with football hooligans for bottom place in the affections of the Great British Public; they'd got militant leaders from the Greater London Council and the Liverpool City Council; they'd got a student activist leader from the North London Polytechnic, where he had been studying since the late 'sixties; they had agreed to a speaking engagement for the Labour Party Leader, and had agreed that they would even accept a visit from the Deputy Leader, if Labour Party HQ insisted. It was all, as Jerry said, "falling into place."

So when, next day, the candidates assembled at a
Methodist Hall hired by the Bootham East Labour Party,
Jerry did not bother to go through the sort of depre-
catory disclaimers that Antony Craybourne-Fisk had
gone in for. He stood there, tall, broad-shouldered,
red-shirted, certain in his certainties, and he made no
attempt to hide the fact that he was going to be the
Labour candidate. The other six people who (for form's
sake) were to go before the General Management
Committee—five men and a woman who didn't seem
to know why she was there—milled around him, re-
sentful, bewildered, and out-manœuvred. Sam Quimby,
the soon-to-be-ousted candidate, said to him: "I know
it's just a formality. I know I'm out." Jerry smiled in
a superior way and said: "We'll just have to wait and
see, won't we?"

After the inevitable had happened Sam Quimby, who
in the sentimental jargon of political commentators had
"a lifetime of service to the party" behind him, came
up to Jerry again.

"Well, I don't like the way it was done. I don't like
it at all. But I've been a loyal Labour man all my life,
and I'll not go against my principles now. For what it's
worth, you can have my endorsement as candidate."

"Good of you," said Jerry.

"I'll even, if you want me, come and campaign for
you."

"We'll see if something can be arranged," said Jerry,
positively lordly.

"But I'll tell you this: I would have won this seat;
and you, with your brand of politics, haven't a hope
in hell."

"I don't know that politics is necessarily about win-

ning always," said Jerry, in his "explaining things to
infants" voice. "What matters is that at last we've got
a chance to get real Socialist policies across to the elec-
torate."

This was conventional wisdom in the Workers for
Revolutionary Action movement. What mattered at this
stage was capturing the party machine, and using it to
get a Socialist message across. But though Jerry Snaithe
subscribed to it with his mouth, he did not do so in
his heart. Jerry very much wanted to get elected, and,
having used his friends from the WRA, he now intended to do everything in his power to ensure that he
was. Including, if necessary, ditching his friends. He
was, like Antony Craybourne-Fisk, a real political
animal.

That very evening the *ad hoc*, part-time representative
of the Social Democrats in Bootham East was rung up
by his party leader from the House of Commons.

"I was wondering if you'd done any of the soundings
you promised to do among the local members. About
whether they wanted to keep this local candidate, or
whether we should shunt in one of our national
figures."

"Well, yes, actually, I have," said the representative.
And he had, too. It had not taken him long. The Social
Democratic Party had very few paid-up members in
Bootham East, though as he had told the Party Leader
in an earlier conversation, there were lots and lots of
people who said they might well consider voting Social
Democrat should the opportunity arise.

"First of all, though," the representative went on,

"I don't know if you've heard, but the Labour Party has selected Jerry Snaithe tonight as their candidate."

"Great!" said the Leader, with real enthusiasm. "A splendid bogey-man figure for us. 'Labour Party taken over by extremists,' and all that. It'll be true, too."

"Quite. I thought you'd be pleased. But with one candidate from Conservative Central Office, the other on the GLC—"

"Yes," said the Leader, his voice showing that he knew what was coming.

"I think the general feeling here will be that we should stick with the local man. It could be a winning card . . ."

"Yes," said the Leader again, trying to keep the scepticism out of his voice. "And this Mr—er—"

"Worthing."

"Yes, Worthing, he's a—what?—schoolmaster?"

"A lecturer at the local College of Further Education."

"Of course. What sort of candidate will he make, do you think?"

"He's very engaged, well up in local issues . . . very earnest . . . He *has* been the candidate before, you remember."

"I remember. But without the sort of media exposure he'll get this time. That's the vital point. That can make or break a candidate. Is he a good speaker?"

"Yes—*quite* good . . . A little dull . . . Inclined to be long-winded, in fact . . . But it's quite easy to stop him. I just pull at his sleeve. And he's *very* hard-working. Bones up on the subjects at issue, has all the facts at his fingertips . . ."

"Right," said the Leader, accepting the inevitable.

"Well, that's decided then. Now all we have to do is get the bandwagon rolling and send in the storm-troopers."

It was not a very appropriate image for the leader of the Social Democratic Party to use.

Thus were chosen the candidates for the three main parties for the by-election at Bootham East, the campaign for which was not scheduled officially to begin until February 6th, and which was already promising to be a media-event of some magnitude; several national newspapers had begun drying out their political hacks in preparation, and their editors were sharpening the language of their political invective. Two days later, the *Daily Grub*, in a rare departure from its steady diet of tits, bums and stories about Prince Andrew, printed photographs not only of the three main candidates, but also of the MP whose death ("which has not yet been satisfactorily explained") had caused the by-election. It was this picture of James Partridge that brought the little man from Battersea in to see Superintendent Sutcliffe, and to start questions about James Partridge's death buzzing once more around the corridors of power.

4

Home from Home

Wilfred Dowson was a retired local government clerk who for many years had laboured in various of the bureaucracies of the London County Council and the Greater London Council ("before they were hijacked by this present gang of comedians," he used to say, over a half-pint of shandy). He was a local government official of an old but well-known type in his generation: a deeply conservative Labour voter, he had an encyclopædic knowledge of bye-laws, departmental minutes, sub-sections in standing orders—in fact, he was a master-spider in the vast web of local bureaucracy, and very few were the applicants for handouts from their council who got past his cautious and parsimonious temperament. "Never do anything in a hurry" was his motto, and he ran his little Circumlocution Office in such a way that as often as not this meant: "Never do anything at all."

Now he was retired, and he spent much of his time in Battersea Public Library, not far from his home. It

was warm there, so he saved on heating bills; there
were people there (he had buried his wife, gratefully,
some two years before he retired), so he never felt
lonely; and he could read all the national and local
papers at his leisure, and pursue in the Reference Library some arcane by-way of his favourite hobby, moths.

When Wilfred Dowson saw the picture of James Partridge in the *Daily Grub* for January 21st, he frowned,
puzzled, and thought it over for a day or two. He had
been rather "off colour," as he put it, in early December, and had not got into the library as much as usual.
So now he demanded the back files of *The Times* and
the *Daily Telegraph*, and read what they had had to
say—it was a meagre amount, in fact—about the death
of James Partridge. Then he decided to go to the nearest
local police station. Here there was another hiccup,
because the man on the desk there at lunch-time when
he went in was a PC of more than usual dimness, a
young thug who had only joined the force for a bit of
legitimized violence, and who lived for those times when
he and a few of his mates in blue could put the boot
into blacks, druggies and other weirdos who were what
was laughably described as "resisting arrest." This thick
youth sat at the desk, yawning and scratching his crotch,
and he told Wilfred Dowson that as far as he knew
there wasn't no case, and it didn't come within their
province anyway, and it didn't sound as if there was
much in it, did there? Oh yeah, if he really felt like it
he could go along to Scotland Yard—it wasn't any skin
off *his* nose, was it?

Wilfred Dowson was so incensed at the unenthused
reception of his information that it was only after two

days, and after penning an indignant letter to the Battersea Police peppered with phrases from his local government days ("pursuant to this matter I volunteered information"), that Wilfred put on his raincoat on the morning of the twenty-seventh and trotted over Vauxhall Bridge and down Millbank to New Scotland Yard. Here he mentioned the matter at the desk to a young sergeant who was a very much brighter article; he looked in files, and rang straight up to Superintendent Sutcliffe. Within ten minutes he was sitting in Sutcliffe's office, with its fine view down the Thames, and a constable was bringing him coffee from the Yard canteen. Mr Dowson blossomed. This was more like. This was giving him the importance that he had always known he deserved.

"I saw his picture in the *Grub*," he explained in his precise, punctilious voice. "Not a paper I would normally read, or not normally *buy*, but this was in the reading room, you understand. I was surprised at his having been an MP. So I went and looked up the account of him in the *Telegraph*, and found that he lived with his wife and family in Cardew Walk, Chelsea. That really did take me aback! Because of course he didn't!"

"He didn't?"

"Indeed he did not. He lived in the house next door to me!"

"And where is that?"

"No. 62, Flannagan Road, Battersea. I'm number sixty. Sixty-two is split in half—an upstairs and a downstairs flat. He had the upstairs."

"And how long had he lived there?"

"Not long. Matter of two, perhaps three months."

"And you're quite sure this was James Partridge?"

"Quite sure. Absolutely and without question. I saw him quite often—leaving or coming home. He was a bit of a walker—didn't catch the bus if he wasn't in a hurry, so often I'd be just behind him part of the way, as I went to the shops or the library, and he went—as I *now* realize—towards Westminster."

"You didn't talk to him?"

"Not beyond 'Good Morning' or 'Evening.' "

"But you did see him well?"

"Perfectly well. On countless occasions. And another thing: I used to see him come home at night, very late, and then I'd see his face in the lamplight, as he looked for his key. I keep a good watch on, I do. What with these terrorist cells springing up everywhere—first thing you know you've got a bomb factory next door. Oh, I keep an eye on things, don't you worry!" He leaned forward, to clinch the matter: "*And* I saw the initials on his briefcase—J.S.P."

"James Spenser Partridge."

"That's right. That was in his obituary. Some sort of family connection with a poet. How many J.S.P.s the spitting image of James Spenser Partridge, MP, do you think there are? No, no, no—it was him all right. You can be quite certain of that."

"Well, Mr Dowson," said Sutcliffe ruminantly, stroking down the greying moustache which gave him the look of a pessimistic seal, "I find this information very interesting—puzzling, too . . . Of course, many MPs have a *pied-à-terre*—"

"Not if they have flats in Chelsea, they don't," said Mr Dowson triumphantly.

"Not as a rule. And I've certainly seen the flat in
Chelsea . . . He did *live* there, you say, in the house
next door to you? It wasn't some sort of business office?
He came home every day?"

"He did indeed, except sometimes at weekends.
Constituency business, see. Otherwise he was there
every day: I'd be sure to see him, either morning or
evening. Erratic times, because they don't keep regular
hours there, but I'd see him."

"Do you happen to know the landlord of that house?"

"Not personally, but I know who it is. Lives down
the road at No. 40—Harold Bly, the name is. Inherited
the house when his mother-in-law died, and converted
it into two flats—very tastefully done, I believe. I've
known one or two of the gentlemen who lived there.
He gets in a very nice little rent, so I've heard."

"I think I'd better talk to Mr Bly. If you'd put your
coat on, Mr Dowson, I'll drive you home."

To have saved on his bus fare both ways was pure
heaven to Mr Dowson, but to complete his enjoyment
the adventure would have had not to have ended there.

"I could come along with you and introduce you,"
he said as they drew up at No. 60. In view of his
declared lack of acquaintanceship with the landlord,
this seemed a particularly empty offer. Sutcliffe was an
experienced officer, experienced with civilian ghouls as
well as criminals, but he maintained a tired courtesy
with both. He declined Dowson's offer civilly, and as
he drove off towards No. 40 he imagined Wilfred Dowson taking up position behind the best window in his
house for observation, hoping for sensational devel-
opments.

James Partridge's landlord, if that indeed was what he was, turned out to be fiftyish, paunchy, quite possibly lazy, but not unintelligent.

"I thought it was funny," he said, when Sutcliffe had explained his business.

"What was funny?"

"Well, his just going like that. And his wife explaining that he was dead."

"You've been in contact with the wife?"

"Well, I had to," explained Harold Bly. "See, the rent was paid to December 31st. First day or two after that I didn't think much to it, it being the festive season, and lots of people away with relatives, and so on. But he'd always been a regular payer, the short time he'd been there, so about the sixth or seventh I began to get worried. So I took my key and went along to see that there was nothing amiss. Well, there was and there wasn't. It was all neat and tidy, except for a saucepan which had had boiled milk in it—the remains were all festering. He didn't look the type to go off for a long period and leave that—not by the look of the rest of the flat. Though it was all perfectly shipshape, it was pretty clear he hadn't slept there for some time. Well, I found an old bank statement in the waste-paper basket, with a Chelsea address. I waited a day or two, walked along to see if there was ever any lights on there, and when it was clear he hadn't come back, I wrote to him at this Chelsea address."

"And his wife replied that he was dead?"

"That's right. Said that he had only rented the flat temporarily, due to alterations at their home—though that certainly wasn't *my* understanding—and that un-

fortunately he had died last month. Didn't offer to pay
the January rent. Of course, if I'd read my newspaper
better I might have known he was dead, because he
was here under his own name all right, but I've never
been one for political news, and my paper doesn't have
all that much in anyway."

"Are his things still in the flat?"

"No, they're not. When I got this letter I rang up
Mrs P., to ask whether she'd come round and sort
through them herself. She sounded surprised. It didn't
seem to have occurred to her that he had things there.
I stepped into the breach and said I could load the things
into my car and drive them round to her. She said, 'Oh,
could you be so kind . . . ?' You know the kind of
voice. I said I'd come the next morning, and she said
that might be difficult, and could I make it the
evening—?"

"After dark?"

"Right. Eight o'clock. So that's what I did, and she
took it all in, thanked me, and that was that."

"Gracious," commented Sutcliffe, who had taken
rather a melancholy view of Penelope Partridge from
the beginning.

"Gracious *and* generous," agreed Harold Bly. "I know
the type. Mind you, it was no great fag. There was a
lot of paper—duplicated stuff, and so on—but not a
lot of personal gear at all. More than a change of clothes,
but not his whole wardrobe, if you get me. For all I
know he could still have been living partly at home."

"His next-door neighbour says not," said Sutcliffe.
"And it seems likely he would know. How long, by
the way, had he lived in the flat?"

"Oh, from early in September, so you'd have thought he would have been more settled in than he seemed to have been."

"I begin to think he cultivated anonymity, or was that way by nature. Do you think I could see the flat?"

"Surely," said Harold Bly, fetching his keys.

Not a Conservative MP's road, Sutcliffe had commented to himself as he drove along Flannagan Road. Not a Conservative MP's flat, he thought when Harold Bly let him in. A poky flat in a poky street, watched over by Wilf Dowson next door, and probably by several other lower-middle-class Wilf-Dowson-look-alikes from the other houses around. The flat had been meticulously cleaned, ready for any new tenant, and with that and the removal of his things there was no sign whatsoever left of James Partridge's tenancy. But it still seemed to Sutcliffe, with its "tasteful" redecoration of a decidedly scruffy elderly terrace house, an unlikely place for a Conservative MP, except as a very temporary arrangement. He wondered how to put this tactfully.

"How did Mr Partridge hear about this place?" he asked.

"He just came along and said he'd heard it was vacant. I hadn't advertised, but I didn't think anything of that. These things get around. And I realize now that he must have heard about it from the previous tenant."

"Who was?"

"Terence Stopford. Conservative MP for East Molesworth. Used to have a constituency up North, but it got redistributed, and he got nominated for a seat closer to London. He had this flat as a *pied-à-terre* while he

was living up North. I don't think he was one of the
particularly well-heeled mob, or else he was careful.
Anyway, when he got in in East Molesworth he started
looking around for a house there, so he could move
his family, you see. Eventually he found one and gave
up this place. Drove up to Westminster each day, so
it wasn't necessary. That's how Partridge heard of it,
I'd guess . . ."

"I see. He might be worth talking to. You haven't
got anything you could add, have you? Any personal
impressions? Anything he once said to you that now
seems odd?"

Harold Bly thought, but briefly.

"Nothing. We had very little contact. He dropped
a cheque for the rent through my letter-box as a rule.
I only talked to him at the beginning, and once when
we met in the street—the weather, whether the flat was
proving suitable, nothing more than that. He was a
very quiet, pleasant, unobtrusive kind of person. Never
said anything interesting that I remember."

It was a fair definition, Sutcliffe thought, of one sort
of Tory MP.

"It's puzzling," said Sutcliffe, eyeing his superior with
his melancholy eyes and pulling at his grey, droopy
moustache. "Had he left his wife? If so, why couldn't
she have said so? It's no shame, these days. I feel I've
been fooled."

"You've certainly been strung along," said the Assistant Deputy Commissioner. "And there's every
reason for going along and hauling her over the coals—
wasting police time by withholding information, and

so on. But I don't know about puzzling. Doesn't it give you that motive for suicide that you were lacking?"

"It could, I suppose. But one would have expected it in September, not December. And if he was shattered by the separation, he was managing to keep it very secret from those around him. I feel there's more in this case than meets the eye. Can I have *carte blanche* to nag away at it for a bit?"

"I don't know about that," said the Assistant DC. "As far as I can gather, the PM desperately wants the thing decently buried."

"If we do that at the behest of the PM, we'll have the Opposition baying for our blood as soon as the truth begins to come out. And quite right too."

"True, of course," admitted his superior. "But that doesn't make it less awkward . . . What came out at the inquest?"

"Open verdict. Which was the right one, in my opinion. The doc was very non-committal—some rather ambiguous bruises, especially to the face, less water in the lungs than he would have expected. I don't think he was happy, and I think that's a good deal more important than the political convenience of the PM."

The Assistant DC sat there for a moment, considering. The fact was that, though the Prime Minister was a great and eloquent admirer of the police, the Assistant Deputy Commissioner was (by pure chance) not a great admirer of the Prime Minister. Nor did he think that political pressure should be brought on the police— particularly in a case when a politician was involved. Yet the mere fact that the Prime Minister's views were known meant that political pressure was being brought.

This administration was inclined to interfere with the judicial processes, in ways that the Opposition found it hard to pin down.

"I'll give you a couple of weeks," he said. "I can't see how I could justify more than that. When are you due to retire?"

"March the fifth," said Sutcliffe. He looked at his superior. "I'm due for some leave before then."

His superior looked straight back at him.

"I rather thought you might be. Of course, how an officer spends his leave is not the concern of Scotland Yard. Especially on the eve of his retirement."

Sutcliffe smiled his thanks. The two men understood each other very well indeed.

5

Prying

"As far as I'm concerned, you're prying," said Penelope Partridge, draped resentfully along the length of her Chelsea sofa.

"As far as I'm concerned I'm prying too," said Sutcliffe. "It's a large part of a policeman's job."

"I don't accept that. To be perfectly frank" (she meant that she would like to be very rude indeed), "I don't see what it's got to do with you."

"Come, come, Mrs Partridge," said Sutcliffe, playing his tired-courtesy card, one of his strongest, "a woman in your position can't be ignorant of the purpose of an inquest. It's to determine the cause of death. All relevant facts about the dead man's position and state of mind have to be presented."

"Nonsense. The separation took place in September. It had no relevance at all."

"In fact, if the jury had had this information before it, it might have brought in a suicide verdict, and we would have called the case closed."

A shade of regret wafted across Penelope Partridge's

face, the first he had seen. He leaned forward and rapped out: "As it is, you've put yourself in the position of having lied to the police, both directly and by implication. And that means we simply cannot let the matter rest there."

"I really don't see why not," drawled Penelope Partridge, unfazed.

"If you don't see that lying to the police is a serious matter, then there's nothing more I can say to make you see. I can, on the other hand, ask you to come down to the Yard, to help us with our inquiries." He paused, to let her consider this option. "Or alternatively you can give me a full, a *very* full, account of the separation."

Something very like a pout appeared incongruously on Penelope Partridge's long face.

"I don't see how I can give you a *very full* account. I mean, there is so little to say about it. We got bored—that's the beginning, middle and end of it. We found there was nothing left in the marriage, and we decided to separate. As far as I was concerned, James had become thoroughly boring, the original nowhere man, and I wasn't interested in staying tied to him. No doubt he saw things differently."

"How do you think he saw them?"

Penelope Partridge was clearly about to suggest that he go and ask him, but she pulled herself back in time.

"I imagine he thought that when his ministerial career ended, I lost interest in the marriage. I expect he told himself I was a cold bitch—that's one of the things men do say about women, isn't it?"

"Yes," said Sutcliffe, with something like feeling. "And what about the children?"

"Well, he was intending to take them off my hands as much as possible. It was a trial separation. When and if we made it official—I said I'd do the odd constituency appearance, where it absolutely couldn't be avoided, until Christmas, just in case we either of us changed our minds—he was going to make the cottage in Moreton his main home, and take them there as often as possible. The flat in—where was it?—Battersea was simply a temporary *pied-à-terre*. I suspect it was rather tatty, wasn't it?" She asked that with a contented cat smile, which she seemed immediately to regret. "As it was, he came to see them or took them out quite often, because he was very fond of them."

"There was no other woman?"

She shrugged.

"Not so far as I know. He wouldn't be likely to tell me."

"Nor anyone in your own life?"

"No one at all."

She was looking straight, coolly at him, in a way he found thoroughly untrustworthy.

"Why in fact did you lie about this?" Sutcliffe asked.

"I didn't *tell* you about it to save myself unnecessary embarrassment. Is there anything wrong in that?"

Sutcliffe left a few moments' silence.

"You'd been married—how long?"

"Eight years."

"Why did you marry?"

It was an unconventional question, but one Penelope Partridge had frequently asked herself. Indeed when, a few days before the wedding, a friend had told her that her married name would make her sound like something out of Beatrix Potter, she had damned near called the whole thing off there and then. Perhaps the truth was that she had been twenty-six, had come from a glacially traditional family who regarded that age in the light of "high time she was off our hands," and she had taken the best on offer. But she had collected together in her mind other, slightly more presentable motives.

"James had built up a whole string of businesses almost from nothing. It wasn't very fashionable, that sort of enterprise, then, but I admired him for it. He'd made a good deal of money, and frankly I enjoy money. Only hypocrites pretend not to. At that time Lord Knowles—do you know him?—had a little knot of promising Conservative thinkers and young candidates, and they used to meet regularly at Mertlesham, his place."

"Sort of Cliveden set?" (Sutcliffe pronounced it Clive-den).

"*Cliv*den. Yes. Only less a set than a random assortment. I was into politics myself then, and I was invited along because there were too few women . . . I must have been dazzled . . . though James was not in himself dazzling . . . Anyway, we were married, and happy enough, but somehow after the children were born, and even when his career was going well, he lost interest." She did her characteristic look around the drawing-room, as if it held all that a heart could desire. "I mean, he inexplicably didn't seem to care any more. Don't ask *me* to explain. I never could."

Sutcliffe, on the other hand, thought perhaps he could.

"And you say he came back now and again to see the children?"

"Oh yes. Frequently."

"When was the last time you saw him, then?"

"Oh, Good Lord—I wasn't myself here necessarily when he came to see them. Helga would always be around. It must have been . . . oh, four weeks or more before he died when I saw him last."

"And he seemed—normal?"

"Perfectly normal." She looked at her watch. "And now, I do have an appointment, Superintendent . . . er . . ."

Sutcliffe waited several seconds before he responded.

"I have no more questions." He got up, but added with the merest suspicion of a threat in his voice, "I'll be following things up, here and in Yorkshire. As soon as anything comes up that I need to consult you about, I'll be back."

He looked at her hard.

"Oh—er—yes, of course."

And Penelope Partridge actually rang for him to be shown out. Sutcliffe was pleased to see that the Danish au pair made no effort whatever to fit in with such an olde-world scenario. She bounced through the door, held it open for him, breezily banged it shut, and in the hall, from her six feet one to his five feet ten, winked at him. As they progressed down the hall towards the street door, Sutcliffe heard the drawing-room door open again, and Penelope Partridge walk briskly upstairs. He did not hear her go beyond the landing. He scuffled in his pocket to find one of the cards he always kept there, with his name and Yard extension number on it. At the door he handed it to Helga and mouthed "Ring me." She nodded massively, smiled, and shut the door behind him.

Sutcliffe's car was parked unobtrusively round the corner. As he dawdled thoughtfully down the Chelsea street, thinking of the emptiness from which James Partridge had flown, he saw among the people coming towards him a young man: blue, expensive suit, umbrella, Burberry over his arm, a round, unlovely face set in an expression of some complacence. Nothing remarkable about any of those things; he could have been duplicated many times over in the streets of Chelsea at any hour. And yet the face—hadn't he seen it before? If not in the flesh, then as a photograph. Where? Not, surely, in the Yard's rogues' gallery of portraits. In connection, though, with a case, he felt. And since the young man looked a genuine smoothie, and since his cases seldom involved classes so well-heeled as this one, then didn't he have some vague connection with the Partridge suicide? He turned and looked round. The young man had rung the doorbell of Penelope Partridge's Chelsea house, and was now standing waiting on the step.

When he got back to the Yard he went straight to his file on the case. There, in the identical cutting that had sent Mr Wilfred Dowson along to him, he found what he wanted. Along with the picture of James Partridge whose death "has not yet been satisfactorily explained," he saw staring at him the candidates adopted for the by-election by the three main parties. Among them he recognized the suavely self-absorbed features of Antony Craybourne-Fisk.

The call from Helga came earlier than Sutcliffe had expected, later in the same day.

"She is gone," she announced.

"Gone?"

"To Herod's," said Helga, as if Penelope Partridge was bidden to a party at which the Dance of the Seven Veils might be expected to be performed.

"When can we meet and talk?"

"I finish nine o'clock. I go vid my boyfriend to the pub—the Nelson, off Whitehall. You know?"

"I know."

"You come?"

"I come."

In the interval Sutcliffe spent some time trying to imagine what sort of a figure the boyfriend of the Wagnerian Helga could be. He came up finally with a diminutive Portuguese waiter, on the principle of the attraction of opposites. When he walked into the Admiral Nelson at twenty past nine he found he could not be more wrong. Sitting draped around Helga, the pair of them looking like one of Vigeland's more monstrous imaginings, was an immense young man who looked in his combination of flesh and muscle like an Olympic discus thrower, or a Smithfield porter at least. What bed could hold their couplings, Sutcliffe wondered, as he fetched himself a pint. Most likely they did it at night in Hyde Park, and the earth moved under them. Helga improbably introduced the young man as Seymour, and he sat there saying little but beaming amiably.

"Now, what you want to know?" asked Helga.

"The situation in the household, before and after the separation."

"Before I don't know. I come in September, and he

had moved out already. She say he is busy, important politician, all that stuff. Then a few weeks later, she tell me they have—what do you call it?—trial separation. I say OK—is perfectly usual."

"But he came back fairly often?"

"To see the children, yes. Mostly he take them out —to films, to the park, to tea."

"What was your impression of him?"

Helga shrugged.

"Not very strong. Was a bit—*dempet ned*—subdued. Not so much later when he got use to me. Quiet man, not much personality on the surface, perhaps very strong underneath, I donno."

"You didn't feel he was taking the separation badly?"

"Oh no. Perhaps a relief. He say to me once, 'When Parliament is in re—ré—' "

"Cess?"

"Yes—'recess, then I fix up the cottage in Yorkshire and have the children with me up there.' And I say: 'Good—then I have more time free.' "

Helga and Seymour indulged in giant panda embraces that threatened to overturn the small table they were all sitting at.

"What about her?"

"Her?" Helga shrugged. "Cold, snobbish, selfish— you see her, you judge. She is always the same. Can't hide it. Not the intelligence to see what impression she make, or maybe she don't care."

"Is she having an affair?"

Helga thrust out her lower lip.

"Affair. Affair. Who knows? She is having *some*-thing. Yes, I think she is probably having an affair."

"Who with?"

"This young man with the fishy name."

"Antony Craybourne-Fisk?"

"That's right. She try to make me announce him, but I always get the name wrong in intention, so she stop me. Fishy name, fishy nature."

"Has this been going on since you took the job?" Helga considered.

"I donno. You see, not much is going on at all, so when it start I'm not sure. Very low-temperature romance, like people think the British always have. They never sleep together at the flat, you know. So when it start, I can't really say."

"Where do they sleep together, then?"

"Outside," said Helga. Sutcliffe looked puzzled for a moment. Hyde Park was one thing for Helga and her boyfriend, quite unthinkable for Penelope Partridge and hers.

"She means away from home," explained Seymour.

"That's right. He rings. And then three or four hours later—*very* clever, Mrs Partridge—she says, 'Oh, Helga, I shall be away for the weekend,' and gives me *very* generous time off in compensation. Which gives the game away, because Mrs Partridge is *not* generous by nature, oh, by no means!"

"Does he come round often to the house?"

"Before, fairly often. Recently, not. Today the first time for—oh, two, three weeks. They talk on the telephone."

"And do you hear what they say on the telephone?" Helga giggled, like Isolde in skittish mood.

"Of course. She has a loud voice when she talk into the telephone, like she was calling to dogs."

"What do they talk about?"

"Well, sometimes they plan these . . . meetings."

"Dirty weekends," said Seymour, as if he were supplying a technical term to a novice.

"Yes. Then the voice goes very low—so equally I *know*. Otherwise she talk normally. The other day what they talk about is this hut in Yorkshire."

"Cottage," said Seymour.

"What did they say about that?" asked Sutcliffe.

"She said: 'Well, if it gets too awful at the hotel, you can always borrow the cottage.' " (Helga's imitation of her voice was not too accurate, suggesting that Denmark did not boast of too many of the Penelope Partridge type). "Then she say 'Wise? That's for you to decide. I can't see anybody commenting if you say that the widow of the late member has let you borrow the place. *I* shan't be using it, that you can be sure of. It's in the hands of the agents, but until it's sold it's yours to use if you want it.' Only I think she said 'at your disposal,' which makes it sound like garbage."

"And did he accept?"

"I don't know. I think they leave it up in the sky."

"Air," said Seymour.

Sutcliffe bought them both enormous tankards of lager, enlisted Helga as a spy for any future happenings of interest in the Partridge household, and then went on his way. The case was beginning to *be* a case, beginning to get accretions, have reverberations. He was beginning to think he might be able to justify a trip up to Yorkshire.

While he was clearing out his desk next morning, Sutcliffe had an important phone call. He knew it was important because of the number of people who spoke to him before the caller himself actually came on. It was, a Roedean voice informed him, from Conservative Central Office, the Chairman himself who wanted to have a talk (quite informally, of course) with him.

"Superintendent Sutcliffe?" said the Chairman, trying to sound like a serious politician.

"Yes."

"Look, you know the last thing we'd do is interfere with a genuine police investigation. But this really does seem over the edge. The PM is absolutely livid, I can tell you. Apparently you've been positively harassing the poor little widow of James Partridge. Now, really, I *can't* think that can be necessary. In fact, I thought the whole business was dead and buried. Why isn't it? I tell you, with the by-election starting officially in a week, dragging this thing out as you are doing begins to seem politically motivated."

"Does it, sir? I'm sorry about that."

"Well, it does. Yes, it does—to the PM too, let me tell you. I mean, this poor lady, Mrs . . . er . . . Partridge, in the stress of the moment, fails to mention that she and her husband were temporarily living apart. And now, five or six weeks after he dies, you feel fit to take the matter up. I mean to say, does it matter?"

"We think it does, sir. And it's not just that."

"No?" (A faintly hollow sound to that "no?")

"You don't, I suppose, approve of lying to the police, sir?"

"Good heavens, Superintendent, you know that our party—"

"Mrs Partridge lied to the police about several matters. That she assumed her husband had gone to his separate bedroom, and so on."

"Little things, Superintendent. In the stress of the moment."

"The statements were repeated at the inquest, sir. And there's another thing—"

"Yes?"

"This is in confidence, sir. Though of course you may repeat it to the PM if you think fit."

"Ye-e-es."

"We are investigating a connection—a *close* connection, if you understand me—"

"Yes."

"—between Mrs Partridge and another politician in your party."

"But, good heavens, Superintendent—of course morality in domestic life is absolutely vital, but in this day and age—"

"The gentleman is your candidate for the constituency of Bootham East."

"Oh Lor'," said the Chairman.

6

Campaigning (I)

The Unicorn Hotel had acquired a new attraction since Antony Craybourne-Fisk's first visit at the time of his selection. In the dining-room there was now a Sicilian called Gianni: sallow, with black crinkly hair and appalling teeth, he exuded self-love. He toted a dangerous pair of eyebrows at Antony on the first morning as he took his order for bacon and eggs, and he toted them again when he brought him two boiled eggs and a rasher of bacon on a separate plate.

"Oh, for God's sake," muttered Antony, but he did not send them back. It was unlikely that Gianni would prove to be a constituent of his—or indeed that he would ever go so far towards expressing approval of anyone other than his delectable self as to put a cross by their name on a voting slip—but Antony was in a hurry. Antony had a campaign to begin.

Antony had fought a seat before, a hopeless constituency in East London (though not as hopeless, he said to himself, as Bootham East was in every respect except its winnability as a parliamentary seat). If Antony was willing to put himself in his agent's hands, at least for the first days of the campaign, it was not through inexperience, but because he felt himself here on *terra incognita*, a Captain Cook among natives who might turn out to be friendly or unfriendly, but who looked horribly *other*. Thus, when Harold Fawcett said they were going to spend the day touring the constituency with the loudspeaker van, getting out now and then at auspicious spots to meet the natives, Antony acquiesced.

"It'll give people a chance to get to know you," Harold said.

"Quite," said Antony. And me a chance to see the constituency, he thought, with a sinking feeling in his stomach. But it couldn't be put off for ever.

And so they drove, down from campaign headquarters into City Square ("We all know this is a government that has set its sights on the right targets," boomed Antony, in a voice that had somehow acquired a classless ring), along the High Street and up towards Kitchener Road ("with a leader whose courage and firmness is admired the world over"); from Kitchener Road into the new private estate of Arden Grove, with its shoddy houses with ridiculous pimples pretending to be bay windows ("I don't deny we've had to take difficult decisions, even unpopular ones"), and from the mortgaged horror of Arden Grove into the borderline respectability of early postwar council estates in Raynwood Terrace, Raynwood Crescent, Raynwood Avenue and so on, testament to the poverty of imagination of the council officers who had dreamed up the estate ("I realize that many of you are not having it easy, but

would you respect a government that bought you off
with cash handouts?"). That last bit was unwise: many
of the inhabitants of Raynwood estate would certainly
vote for a government that bought them off with cash
handouts.

On they went. From Raynwood View they de-
scended into Somertown Fields, a council estate of flats
and houses constructed with untried materials in the
early 'sixties, and already rickety with numberless ail-
ments, physical and social. Antony, seated on top of
his open van, gazed around him with barely concealed
horror at the boarded-up dwellings, at the gardens
crammed with disused cars, at the front doors ripped
off their hinges, at acres of broken bottles, discarded
lemonade cans, sweet wrappers, broken toys and old
clothes ("What this government represents is the possibility of a new start"). Men in pyjama tops or dirty
T-shirts barely covering monstrous bellies stood idly
smoking in doorways, while women lounged round
seedy shops cackling as they gossiped, and filthy children played in the gutters and jeered at passing cars.

"Here," said Harold Fawcett to the van driver; "we've
come beyond constituency boundaries. This bit's
Bootham South, not Bootham East."

"Bloody fool. Turn around. Let's get out of here,"
said Antony, in tones that were flung electronically all
over Somertown Fields.

Jerry Snaithe was up early, and so were most of his
helpers. His agent's house was too small to act as a
convenient campaign headquarters for such a vital by-
election, so they had rented a largeish house five min-

utes from Bootham's centre. Here they got things just as they liked them. Jerry did most of the directing, watched by Fred Long, the party agent, who had seen candidates come and go, and had seen through most of them. Jerry had brought with him a hard core of party activists from London (who were already raising the hackles of the locals), and he assigned them to various campaign officials, or gave them little rooms and long titles of their own. Five people, led by a bossy lady in spectacles, staffed the main office on the first floor, through which callers could be filtered to the various functionaries for the campaign (Publicity, Meetings, Canvassing, and so on). But before one could even get to the formidable five, one had to get past a gentleman Jerry placed at the bottom of the stairs. An unemployed miner, he was massive and T-shirted, with snakes entering naked ladies tattooed up and down each arm and around his throat, and manners that would have been considered uncouth in nineteenth-century Arkansas. To warn off unnecessary approaches to this representative of working-class macho at its least acceptable, Jerry had a large notice made for the front door, which read:

NO MEDIA PERSONS ALLOWED
BEYOND THIS POINT
RING BELL AND WAIT

He taped this up with his own hands, and was pleased to be photographed by a media cameraperson as he did so. When all this preparation had been completed, Jerry stood in the hall with Fred Long and rubbed his hands.

"Right," he said, "now we're ready to go."

"First stop City Square," said Fred. "How do you think we should arrange it?"

"I thought I'd go round for a bit, shake a few hands, then get up on the van and give a five-minute speech."

"Fine. What are you going to talk on?"

"The need for open government," said Jerry.

Oliver Worthing, the candidate of the Social Democratic Party, woke on the first morning of the by-election with a stale taste in his mouth, and a sense of listlessness that seemed to permeate every limb of his body. He had indulged, the previous evening, in a half-bottle of Hungarian Riesling, but surely that could not account for the fact that he was today so lacking in fizz? Perhaps, he told himself, he did not really want to fight the campaign. Perhaps his political ambitions had been sated by fighting Bootham at the General Election. I fought it *quite* well, he told himself, to buck himself up, but maybe once was enough. Then he thought with a sinking heart of the immensely greater media coverage there would be on this occasion. For three weeks politics would mean Bootham. For three weeks he would be a national figure. Please God let me speak *briefly* and to the point, said Oliver to himself. Please God let me not go on.

Why on earth do I, an unbeliever, say "Please God," even in my thoughts? Oliver asked himself. He cast round in his mind for Social Democratic divinities, and composed a short prayer to Shirley. This made him feel much better humoured, and he got up. He washed and shaved and sat unconscionably long on the lavatory

seat. His toilet-roll packet promised him "A New Experience in Toilet Tissues," and he was wondering why
he could remember so little about his earlier experiences
in toilet tissues. The fact that they had left so little
impression made him feel guilty. Almost anything could
make Oliver Worthing feel guilty.

His children, for example: should he phone his children? There was no particular reason why he should
do so on the first day of the campaign: he had phoned
them three days ago, and Wendy, his ex-wife, didn't
particularly like his phoning them too often, though
she never said anything. But would the children expect
it? Would they feel he had failed them if he didn't? He
went on in this way as he prepared a boiled egg and
toast and a mug of instant coffee. By now it was ten
minutes after the time he should have left for campaign
headquarters, so the decision made itself.

Arriving late at the decrepit first-floor offices due for
demolition that had been loaned free to the SDP by a
local businessman in a passing fit of "a plague on both
your houses," Oliver Worthing found that everybody
else had got there early and was frantically busy. Whether
anybody was co-ordinating with what anybody else
was doing, or whether they really knew what they
themselves were supposed to be doing was less clear,
but there was lots and lots of enthusiasm. They were
mostly middle-class young people, few of them obvious
voter-repellants, but Oliver was also pleased to note a
Sikh, a couple of disaffected miners, and a middle-aged
lady who would almost certainly turn out to be a
spokesperson for gay rights. Good, thought Oliver: a
representative cross-section.

Finding out what he was supposed to be doing was more difficult. Finally they decided to do the obvious thing at this stage in the campaign—tour the constituency with a loudspeaker, and then set up an impromptu meeting somewhere central. One of the miners proved an excellent driver, knowing the constituency like the back of his hand. The only problem was to get him to drive slowly. A very tiny zing entered Oliver's veins as they went from street to street: this was his place, he had lived here for years, and by God the people needed something doing for them. When by chance their paths crossed with Jerry Snaithe's loudspeaker van, Oliver managed to get in a cheeky "You don't want a carpet-bagger in this constituency, do you?" and then added, for good measure: "Well, you're in luck, because you can give two of them a good kick up the pants on February 27th." And when Jerry Snaithe countered with "I'm the only candidate who's fighting this election on the *issues*," Oliver saw several people in the street groan. For a bit he felt quite good. The zing was perceptibly increasing.

They had the impromptu meeting outside the Corn Exchange. Oliver did his usual stuff about "Time for a change—people are sick of Tweedledum and Tweedledee—extremists in control in both parties" and so on. Then he asked for questions. There was by now quite a good little knot of spectators, and a man at the back of them shouted, "Are you in favour of closing down uneconomic pits?"

Oliver knew the right answer to that one; it was "yes." It was the short answer too. It might not please the questioner, or the miner who'd driven him round, but it was the honest answer. But it was also a harsh one, and Oliver had never found it in him to be a harsh man.

"This is an appalling dilemma," he began. "We have to weigh up the social factors, the dereliction of mining communities with their age-old traditions and solidarities . . . whereas on the other hand, the community as a whole, which has to bear the economic costs, has the right to expect . . ."

As Oliver went on, and on, and on, the little knot of spectators evaporated, to go about their everyday business.

"Mother?" said Antony Craybourne-Fisk.

"Yes, who is it?"

"You only have one child, Mother."

"Oh, *An*tony," said Virginia Mavrocordatos, known to her friends and her wine-merchant as Ginny. "How *are* you?"

"Fine. Mother, I'm standing."

"You're what, dear?"

"I'm standing for Parliament."

"Oh, Par-li-a-ment. I thought . . . What on earth are you doing *that* for, darling?"

"Well, it's the sort of thing one does."

"Not *now*adays, darling. Nobody does. It's a positive hothouse of mediocrity. And the dress-sense of the members! Well, if you must, I suppose. It must be your father coming out in you."

"I didn't know father was political."

"But of course he was, darling. Member for . . . that Midlands place, wherever it was."

"That was Harold, Mother. Your second."

"Oh, of *course*, darling."

"Best to get the little details right. Mother, I was wondering about Granny."

"*Who?*"

"Granny Masterson. Your mother."

"Oh, Mumsie."

"I was wondering: is she all right?"

"What on earth are you suddenly wondering about her health for? You haven't seen her for years."

"It's just that this constituency I'm standing for is in Yorkshire. Wasn't Granny Masterson born in Yorkshire?"

"Yes darling . . . Wakefield, can you believe it? And she was in rep there for positive *ages*—Sheffield, or Rotherham, or Darlington, or somewhere like that."

"Better and better. Is she all right?"

"Of course, dear. As far as I know."

"Not senile or an alcoholic or anything?"

"Of course not, dear."

"How long is it since you saw her?"

"*Saw* her? Oh, positive ages. But I spoke to her on her last birthday—or was it the one before?"

"And she sounded all right?"

"*Per*fectly all right. Positively spry. We had a good slanging match, so I know."

"Splendid. Right. And she's still in that home?"

"Oh yes. Arthritis, but otherwise perfectly splendid. An old trouper. I've got the number here somewhere . . . Torquay 48751. Give her my love if you ring."

"Right. Well, 'bye, Mother."

" 'Bye, darling. You don't want me to come up?"

"No, Mother. Love to Peter."

"Takki, darling."

"I beg your pardon?"

"Takki. Best to get the little details right. I'm married to Takki Mavrocordatos. I sent you a card."

"I believe you did."

"Be nice to him, if you should run into him, darling. He's a sweetie, and at my time of life one has to be grateful . . ."

"Meaning he's about my age?"

"I didn't say *that*, darling. But if you *should* run across him—"

"I'll be nice," said Antony, vowing to undertake the longest journey rather than run across Takki Mavrocordatos. "I will, Mother. See you some time. Be good, darling."

"Oh Antony—too late!"

"Sue?"

"Oh, Jerry. How's it going?"

"Terrific. Absolutely terrific. Tremendous enthusiasm. You can tell people here aren't going to take any notice of that 'Red Jerry' stuff the media are putting out. The media are here in droves, by the way."

"That'll please you."

"I was just ringing, Sue, about this business of your coming up here."

"Oh, yes."

"When we talked last you were a bit vague about when you would come."

"No, I wasn't. I was vague about if I would come."

"Come off it, Sue. You know I'm as anti as could be this idea of turning the by-election into a beauty parade or a Happy Families game, but—"

"But?"

"But you know what the Tory press is like: they're going to seize on the least little thing. And your not appearing wouldn't be a little thing in their eyes."

"I've no objection to helping you, Jerry. I think you'd make a very good MP of a certain type. But—"

"Fine. Then shall we say a spot of canvassing the weekend after next, and then a little speech at a meeting, say a week or so before polling day?"

"You ignored my 'but,' Jerry. You always ignore other people's 'buts.' "

"People have too many 'buts.' Nothing but wholehearted commitment is good enough for me."

"Well, you should try and hide that for the next three weeks. Ordinary people don't commit themselves wholeheartedly. My 'but' is that I'm snowed under with work here, the dining-room table is laden down with five separate piles of case files. With these government cuts I'm being handed cases that—"

"Fine. Who better to make that point to people than you? I've got to raise your sights, Sue. You could make a really powerful plea for the sort of people a social worker comes in contact with."

"Meanwhile Jenny Waddel half-starves from Saturday to Monday because her mum's on her own and she's a hopeless manager; Jimmy Cross gets burned with cigarette ends because his dad's a sadist; old Mrs Farraday dies of hypothermia because—"

"Sue—do you think I don't know about all this? Good God, haven't I spent my political life fighting for people like them?"

"I don't know, Jerry. Really, I don't know."

"I want you here, Sue. Do you get me? I'm the only

major candidate who's married, and it could be a big plus in my favour. I don't want any questions. This is a thing that's tremendously important—to us. Do you understand?"

There was a pause.

"Yes, Jerry. I understand."

Antony Craybourne-Fisk had had a hard day. He had shaken innumerable hands, patted the heads of babies (it was very *vieux jeu* to kiss them), had bellowed out uplifting slogans and poured out standard answers to predictable questions. This was his first encounter with broad Yorkshire, and sometimes his answers had been to questions quite different from the ones actually asked. Then in the evening he and Harold had mulled over the arrangements for the press conferences that began on Monday. Central Office had volunteered a whole array of cabinet ministers, to mark their sense of the importance of this by-election. The trouble was, the cabinet was composed almost exclusively of the dullest members of the parliamentary party. They had to get a leavening of bright sparks, but most of those were out of favour with Central Office. It was grinding work, and taxed Antony's powers of diplomacy to their limits. By nature Antony was a scrapper, and a dirty one, not a diplomatist.

When he arrived back at the Unicorn it was quarter to eleven. Thank God, just in time for a drink. Behind the bar, he was disgusted to find, was that same Gianni who had served him breakfast.

"A double Scotch."

Gianni had only two or three words of English, and

had no intention of learning more. He stood there, eyelashes pointed with deadly precision.

"Whisky! Whisky, for God's sake!"

Ah yes. Whisky was one of the words Gianni knew. He uttered some Sicilian apparently signifying that as a favour to the gentleman he would fetch it.

"Double," said Antony. And then, rather daringly, "*Ancora*." He slapped down a fiver, and waited for Gianni to improvise some change.

He took a gulp at his whisky, then looked around the bar. Nobody. Utterly empty. He downed the glass, and then shoved it across the bar. Once more Gianni uttered in Sicilian, and once more as a favour he got the whisky. Antony gave him this time what he thought was a reasonable price, and with a shrug Gianni accepted.

When he had drained his glass a second time it was eleven o'clock. He got off his bar stool, and made for the door. By the door stood Gianni waiting to lock up. As Antony brushed past him, he took him by the arm and—Antony could have sworn—suggested that there was a further favour that he could do the gentleman, if the gentleman was so inclined. Antony gazed with horror at the eyelashes, now delicately fluttering.

"No," he almost shouted. "No!"

When he got to his room he locked the door and lay on his bed. A momentary thought had struck him that "*No*" in Italian might mean "yes," just as "*caldo*" meant "hot." My God—that *would* be a way to begin a by-election campaign! He'd have to get out. He'd have to move to Penny's cottage. He'd ring her tomorrow and arrange it.

7

Country Cottage

When Sutcliffe arrived in Bootham, he was three days short of the two weeks' grace his boss had given him.

"Expecting to find anything?" the Assistant Deputy Commissioner had asked him.

"Not in three days," Sutcliffe had said.

"After that you've got leave, haven't you?"

"That's right."

"Got any particular plans?"

"Yorkshire in February is said to be lovely," said Sutcliffe, and they had both smiled a smile of complicity.

When he drove his car towards Bootham centre it was only half past ten, but already the electoral frenzy that according to the media was gripping the town seemed to have moved to the residential outskirts. The odd cameraman he saw, the odd mangy reporter waiting for the pubs to open, but otherwise people seemed to be going about their everyday business with scarcely a thought for the momentous decision they were to make

on February 27th. Sutcliffe parked his car, looked around
the town unenthusiastically, and then chose a modest
but not too grimy-looking hotel, and went in to
Reception.

They looked at him as if he were mad.

The expression was reproduced on the faces of all
the other reception clerks he approached, except for
those who gazed at him with frank contempt.

"Don't you realize," said one, "that all the world is
looking to Bootham at the moment? You won't get a
room here, not for love nor money. Far as the hotels
are concerned, this is the best three weeks of our lives.
The pubs are coining it hand over fist too. The focus
of all eyes, that's what we are."

"The cynosure," said his assistant complacently,
spreading the word out as if it were caviare.

"You'd best get in your car and try Rotherham or
Sheffield," advised the first.

But Sutcliffe didn't do that. He got out his map of
Yorkshire and hunched over it to read the small print.
He had got a fair idea of the area covered by Partridge's
constituency from *The Times Guide to the House of
Commons*, and he was looking for a place called Moreton within its boundaries. Finally he found a Moreton-
in-Kirkdale which he decided must be the village where
the Partridges had their cottage. He went back to his
car and set off.

That wasn't altogether easy. It was rumoured in
Bootham that the town's traffic system, designed by
the anti-car sadist in the Town Hall, had already cost
the sanity of ten journalists. Certainly one had been
found slumped over the wheel of his car in a horrible

suburb, sobbing in a highly emotional manner. When Sutcliffe eventually discovered a way out, he also found he was not going in the direction of Moreton-in-Kirkdale, but with a bit of intelligent map-reading he finally made it on to the right road.

Moreton-in-Kirkdale was three or four streets, probably about five or six miles as the crow flies (if it was allowed to fly) from the outer suburbs of Bootham. Somewhere in these three or four streets, or in the straggle of cottages beyond, was presumably the Partridges' cottage. There were two pubs, and outside one of them there were a couple of cars with London registration plates. The late-comers among the journalistic contingent, Sutcliffe thought to himself. A board outside advertised PUB FOOD, with underneath: ROOMS. HOMELY ATMOSPHERE. FAMILY HOLIDAYS. That, presumably, was the role the Happy Dalesman had seen for itself before the Bootham area became the cynosure of the world's eyes. Sutcliffe pushed his way into the Saloon Bar, and asked the landlord if he had a spare room.

"Well, we do—just the one single. It is a single, is it?" The landlord looked at him cunningly. "It'll cost you £28 a night, but for that you get a full English breakfast."

Things had come to a pretty pass, Sutcliffe thought, when something that one would only recently have taken for granted was offered as an extra of unimaginable luxury. The price was clearly ludicrous—upped sky-high and higher by the by-election. He took it, and accepted a key on a rusty twist of wire from the landlord.

The room was a box, with a bed and a washstand
and a Gideon Bible. The lavatory was down the end
of a creaking corridor, so that all and sundry could
chart the state of one's bowels and bladder. All the
walls had been distempered in pale green shortly after
the Second World War, it seemed, and the Breakfast
Room was another little box into which eight or nine
tables had been fitted by some kind of conjuring trick.
It was as bleak and comfortless as could be imagined.
"Family" and "homely" here could only have the sort
of connotations they have in the novels of Ivy Compton-
Burnett. If journalists were often posted off to dumps
like this, perhaps they had good reason for going on
the booze. Really there was nothing for it but to go
back to the bar, which probably was the whole point.

The lunch-time rush had not started, but there were
already two or three men whom Sutcliffe couldn't see
as locals, crouched over beer or whisky. Sutcliffe ordered beer and a ham sandwich. ("You won't wait for
our steak and veg pie? It's on at twelve. Very tasty."
Sutcliffe shook his head.) When they came he took them
over to a table under the window.

"Give the canvassing a miss today, did you?" said
the man in the corner—shabby, pot-bellied, with a
pink complexion and hands perpetually grimed from
reading too much newsprint. Sutcliffe nodded non-
committally. "Very wise. You see the bastards doing
one morning's canvass, you've seen the lot. It writes
itself after that. Woman slams door in Labour candidate's face. Pensioner shouts obscenities at Conservative candidate. You don't need to follow the smarmy
bastards round to get stuff like that."

"Home Secretary's coming tonight," said another man at the next table. "Might liven things up a bit."

"You can't have heard him speak, mate. The school prig addressing the school debating society, that's his style. Things won't liven up till we get Tony Benn here. Then we can lay on all the 'red menace' stuff."

The bar, which did not seem to have been properly cleaned for days, was full of broadsheets and handouts scattered in profusion on tables, chairs and floor: the daily Conservative newssheet, the Labour equivalent, notices of meetings, polemics on specific issues, rushed duplicated sheets trumpeting or discounting the latest opinion poll results. Sutcliffe's eye was taken by a collection of the election addresses of each of the main candidates, on the back of which were their potted campaign biographies, printed in the appropriate colours. He made a collection of the three main parties' efforts, and began to read them.

"Old stuff that, mate," said his pot-bellied reporter friend. "Been out all of three days."

"Interesting, though," said Sutcliffe, and so in their way they were.

ANTONY CRAYBOURNE-FISK was born in Norfolk, and educated at Stowe, where he captained the second eleven at cricket, and was an enthusiastic squash player. After graduation from Trinity College, Oxford, he studied law and later went into the City. He still has extensive interests in the Stock Exchange, and in Public Relations, but he has worked since 1980 for Conservative Central Office. He plays a keen game of squash, and is "unmarried but hopeful," as he puts it.

The details given seemed almost designed to show Craybourne-Fisk as the archetype of the "young shit" type in right-wing politics. But if that was what the young man was, and what he had done, it would have been difficult to avoid saying it. He turned to the hand-out of his main rival:

JERRY SNAITHE was born in London, but went to school in Yorkshire. After university, where he graduated in Forestry, he became Labour member for Fordham on the GLC in 1978, becoming Opposition spokesman on housing the next year. When Labour took control in 1980, he became chairman of the important Arts and Leisure Activities Committee. In this position he has tried to rob the Arts of their elitist image, and has financed a variety of popular and community activities. He is thirty-six, and married to a social worker in the borough of Hackney.

"You know what that about robbing the Arts of their elitist image means, don't you?" asked the pot-bellied reporter.

"I can guess," said Sutcliffe.

"It means subsidizing steel bands and pigeon fanciers and working men's clubs and the Tottenham Hotspur fan club."

"Generally giving the ordinary citizen the idea that his tastes are as good as anyone else's? Making the world safe for the reader of the *Daily Grub*?"

"Watch it, mate. I represent the *Daily Grub*."
Sutcliffe cooled it, and went on to the last handout.

OLIVER WORTHING, your *local* candidate, was born
in Rotherham in 1934, where he attended the Primary
and High Schools during and after the war. He did
National Service in Aden and Cyprus, and went to
Hull University, where he studied History and Eco-
nomics. He came to Bootham as Tutor in Community Studies at the College of Further Education
in 1972, and has served on the Town Council since
1978. He stood for the Alliance at Bootham East in
the last election, when he doubled the Liberal vote
at the previous one. His motto is: double it again!
He is divorced, and has three children.

"Nothing there, see," said the pot-bellied *Daily Grub*
reporter. "All old stuff."
"I suppose so," said Sutcliffe thoughtfully. "These
things are always interesting for what they don't say."
The reporter chuckled cynically, as if Sutcliffe was
referring to the candidates' sex lives, but then he thought
and said: "Mean anything by that?"
Sutcliffe shrugged.
"You notice Craybourne-Fisk 'was educated,' whereas
Snaithe 'went to school.' But what school? If it was the
Swardale Comprehensive or something, you'd think
Snaithe would say, wouldn't you? And you'd think
that would mean that he actually *lived* in Yorkshire
as a child, which you'd also think he'd say. Could it
be that *he's* a public schoolboy too, but doesn't want

it known? . . . And then there are the gaps in his
career . . ."

"Gaps?"

"Apparently he went on the Greater London Council in 1978, eight years ago. He was then twenty-eight.
What had he done between university and then? It says
'after university,' but people don't leave university at
twenty-eight, unless they've been doing one hell of a
post-graduate course. That 'after university' could cover
a multitude of sins."

"Worth looking into," said *Grub*, taking out an ap-
propriately grubby little notebook.

"Then, who are Craybourne-Fisk's parents? He thinks
it worth while giving Stowe and Trinity a plug, but
keeps quiet about his parentage. If he's going for some
kind of snob vote, you'd think he'd mention them. And
I wonder what *exactly* he does for a living, apart from
slogging away at Conservative Central Office . . ."

"What about the Alliance man?"

Sutcliffe paused.

"Ah—there it's more difficult. It doesn't seem to be
a life packed with incident, does it? Being a local man,
he'd have a lot more difficulty hiding anything, wouldn't
he? If there was anything about the divorce it would
probably have surfaced at the last election—and, besides, there never *is* anything about divorce these days:
it's so clean and easy."

"Too right, mate. They've nearly been the death of
muck-racking, have the new divorce laws. Hell for the
profession."

"Quite. No—I fear that Mr Worthing is this election's Mr Nice Guy, without any skeletons in his cup-
board. Unless I'm being very naive."

Sutcliffe drained his glass.

"Here—" said the other—"you're not a reporter, are you? I thought you were, but you're not."

"How do you know?"

"Reporters don't give away their ideas, like you've been doing. Not unless they're green, and you're too old to be green. We don't *share* stories in this trade."

"No. Reading the *Grub* I never feel the interplay of several brilliant minds."

"What's your interest in this, then—?"

But Sutcliffe had gone. He slipped into the Public Bar, and got from the landlord the location of the Partridge cottage: down to the end of the main street, then the first turning on the left—a lane that had a couple of stone cottages at the end of it, a matter of fifty yards or so from the main street. Up for sale it was, the landlord believed. Was the gentleman interested?

"*In*terested," said Sutcliffe gnomically—but it was truthful, so far as it went.

When he turned off the principal thoroughfare of Moreton-in-Kirkdale (which had a butcher's, a small supermarket and an all-purpose clothes shop), he slowed down his pace, so as to approach the cottage in a leisurely way, gazing at it with considering eyes. The first of the two stone buildings had the look of still being a countryman's home, but the second of them, the Partridges', had the distinct air of being a "cottage" rather than a cottage—something adapted to the townsman's needs, and the townsman's idea of necessary comforts, even in the country. Mrs Partridge, he felt sure, didn't come out into the country to *work* like a country-woman. The house itself, he eventually realized, was in fact two two-up-two-downers, made into one rea-

sonably large house. It was built of good stone, and
both it and the garden were kept in good order. Partridge would have wanted that, as long as he was the
local MP, and his widow no doubt kept the gardener
on, for the benefit of potential buyers.

His approach, he should have realized, had been observed. One's approach always was observed in the
country. A woman's head popped up from behind the
hedge of the first of the cottages.

"I saw you lookin' at the cottage. Was you the gentleman Mrs Partridge said ud be comin'?"

"Very possibly," said Sutcliffe, which was also truthful as far as it went. He had mentioned to Mrs Partridge
that he might be pursuing the case in Yorkshire.

"Ah—she said a gentleman ud be comin' to 'ave a
look, with a view to movin' in, just until it's sold.
That'd be you, then. I'll just get you the key. I hope
you like it, sir. Always nice to have someone near,
that's what I say, and since my Albert died it's always
felt that bit lonely here. Be glad when the house is sold,
that's for sure, so long as it's not these weekenders,
like before. Though *Mr* Partridge, he was a lovely man,
God rest him. You'll find it's very nice in there, sir,
beautiful furniture, and that . . . Here you are, then,
that's for the front."

She had fetched the key from a nail inside her front
door, and Sutcliffe took it and made off from her gar-
rulity, promising himself a chin-wag with her later if
it seemed likely to repay the trouble. The cottage was
set back somewhat from the lane, and surrounded by
the inevitable privet. The front garden was lawn and
roses, cut back but not yet pruned; round the back he
could see pear and plum trees. The front door was

newly painted dark blue and the paintwork around the windows was spruce. Sutcliffe let himself into the cottage.

The downstairs of the two little houses had been entirely refashioned; the front door now led into a small hallway, with on one side a small dining-room, and on the other a very good-sized drawing-room. Both of them had been furnished on the good old principle of "See Maples and die," but it was the rooms that had died. Large pink plush sofas and chairs declared their domination of the space, heavy oak tables and chairs rendered human beings an intrusion in the dining-room. Penelope Partridge's choice, Sutcliffe surmised: her tastes could not be adapted to a cottage setting. Behind the dining-room there was a kitchen and scullery, and here there were a washing- and a washing-up machine, and a dominating fridge and deep-freeze. There was a breast-high Husqvarna oven, as little cottage-like as it was possible to imagine. Oh, the simple life for me, thought Sutcliffe. In the deep-freeze there was a series of little foil dishes, labelled *Lepre in Agrodolce*, *Stufatino alla Romana*, and so on.

Like the index to an Elizabeth David book, Sutcliffe thought to himself. Was Penelope Partridge bequeathing all these as a rich gift to the gentleman who was coming, or to the cottage's purchaser? Or had she, in fact, not been here since her husband's death? The cottage was extremely tidy (and could never have had much of a lived-in feeling), but when he peered into the waste-paper basket, it was full of duplicated Parliamentary handouts, trivial letters dated late November or early December, and advertising circulars. Presumably someone had been in to clean—the next-door neigh-

bour, very probably—but she had not liked to throw
away anything remotely personal. Why? Sutcliffe wondered. The open verdict at the inquest, perhaps. Intelligent woman! His eye honed in on a little cabinet that
obviously folded out to make a writing desk. He went
over and opened it up.

Inside were the remains of James Partridge's last
weekend's work as MP for Bootham. Letters from constituents were paper-clipped together with carbon copies of Partridge's replies. Looking under the cabinet,
Sutcliffe found stored away the machine on which they
had been typed—an old portable Olivetti. To read
through the letters was to get a vivid sense of an MP's
job and the mental strain of it if he were conscientious
and compassionate, as apparently James Partridge was.
The letters alternated between the silly and the sad, and
even many of the silly ones had an undertone of sadness
—exposing the inadequacy, the panic, the frustration
of small minds caught up in a web of misery in a town
plagued by unemployment and the accumulation of years
of industrial decay. There were small problems that had
mounted up into big ones, there was bafflement at the
ways and words of officialdom, there were personal
difficulties compounded by the misery of poverty and
idleness. James Partridge's replies were models of quiet
helpfulness or regret at helplessness, but once or twice
Sutcliffe sensed, coming through the flat prose, a wail
of frustration at the wretchedness which lay at the heart
of his constituency's problems.

But there was only one letter that seemed of relevance
to Sutcliffe's investigation. It was headed, in embossed
print, Manor Court Farm, Ltd, Cordingate, Bootham,

Yorkshire, and it was on a fine paper, neatly typed, doubtless by a secretary. But the signature at the bottom was a large, brutal scrawl, almost in itself a gesture of defiance. The letter read:

Dear Partridge,

What you say is absolute twaddle. The British public wants cheap food and it's firms like this one that make it possible. Conditions here are second to none, and I'm taking legal advice about what you've written about us. You'll soon get a bloody nose if you start sticking it into our affairs, I can tell you. I make a bad enemy. As a life-long Tory it makes me sick that one of your sort should be our MP, with your lily-livered pseudo-scruples. You should be getting business back on its feet again, not trying to bring it to its knees to satisfy your so-called conscience. I tell you, I not only won't be voting for you, but I'm organizing several of the Conservative Association members who have the business interests of the constituency at heart to see if we can't bring about a change of candidate before the next election. That's what your meddling is likely to bring about.

Sincerely,
Walter Abbot

The carbon of Partridge's reply read simply:

Dear Abbot,

I see no point in prolonging this correspondence.

Yours,
James Partridge

Sutcliffe slipped the letters into his inside pocket, had a swift last look around, and then left the cottage.

"You like it?" said the next-door neighbour cheerfully, still in the garden, when he handed over the key.

"Yes. Yes indeed. Very nice."

"All nice stuff they got, though large for the place I always think. They're lucky it's still all there."

"Oh? Why?"

"Nearly had a break-in t'other night. Half twelve or so it was. I don't sleep well, never 'ave done since my man died, so I heard 'em. Got on the phone to the police, but the silly buggers come from Bootham with their sirens goin', and they was clean gone by the time they got here."

"Did you see them?"

"No—no, I didn't. Just lights and shadows like. What I say is—"

But she was interrupted by the phone inside. She had taken the key, and as he was continuing on down the lane, Sutcliffe heard her say:

"Oh, Mrs Partridge. How are you, then? Getting over it? That's right. Well, your gentleman's been to see the house. Very nice gentleman, very nicely spoken . . . No, a middle-aged gentleman. Quite fifty, I'd say. But—"

But Sutcliffe was out of earshot, going down the lane very much quicker than he had come up it.

8

Manor Court

Manor Court Farm (Ltd) was about eight miles from Moreton-in-Kirkdale, apparently situated near a village even smaller than Moreton. Wanting to see it in daylight, Sutcliffe left it till the morning, and spent the evening listening to gossip about the campaign and its personalities from the motley collection of journalists at the Happy Dalesman. These turned out to be mostly from the provincial dailies—Johnnies-come-lately, or men whose editors had tight budgets—with only a sprinkling of men from the nationals—men like the *Grub* reporter, who had come out to Moreton because Bootham was so nasty. There was also a melancholy little Spaniard, doing a report for Spanish television, who had been going round Bootham asking people their views on the Gibraltar question, and the London correspondent of a German daily, who seemed to have no more than ten or fifteen words of English, all of them guttural.

The next morning he set out for Cordingate.

The village itself turned out to be fifteen or twenty
cottages and small houses, clutching the side of a hill.
No such village in Yorkshire is entirely lacking in attraction if it is built of the local stone, but there was
about Cordingate something skimped and furtive, as if
it had never had much reason for being there, and apol-
ogized for disturbing the rural calm. It was not the sort
of village that anyone would choose to have a country
cottage in—not even a Conservative MP whose constituency gave him a limited choice in the matter. Sutcliffe inquired at the village shop the way to Manor
Court Farm, and after driving half a mile on tarmac,
turned off on to a rough track that soon landed him
up outside a large and heavy farm gate.

That gate, in fact, was the most conventionally rustic
thing about Manor Court Farm, though its Constable-
esque quality was impaired by a notice which read:

MANOR COURT FARM LTD
NO ADMISSION EXCEPT ON BUSINESS
RING BELL AND WAIT

Sutcliffe got out of his car, rang the bell, and waited,
leaning in a traditionally rural pose across the gate,
taking in what little he could see of Manor Court Farm.

What had once been the farmhouse was now merely
a wing to a solid and assertive main block, which faced
the gate and said "Here I am" in a tremendous manner
to the visitor. It was red-brick and regular, in a vaguely
eighteenth-century way, with its porched main door
set in the middle, and the windows on both floors
arranged symmetrically around it. It was a dull day,

and through the windows Sutcliffe could see strip lighting in all the rooms. The house fitted its environment about as well as if Wuthering Heights had been set down in the middle of nineteenth-century Manchester.

Beyond the house were long, barrack-like sheds, more like hangars or warehouses. They stretched into the distance, so many of them that one could barely glimpse the fields beyond. They were long, roofed in corrugated iron, and shut in; and from them came very little noise: no warmth, no natural vigour, no sense of the unpredictable, the dangerous, the vital. Sutcliffe was not a fanciful man, but he found the place eerie. More like a concentration camp than a farm, he said to himself.

That door in the centre of what he could only call the admin block opened. The young man who came down to the gate was lithe and jaunty, in a slightly shabby grey suit and a collar and tie that seemed to have been brought together especially to encounter this visitor. The cheeriness of his manner was entirely urban.

"Good morning, good morning. And what can I do for you?"

It was the accent of a cockney barrow boy, whom you might like, but wouldn't trust an inch.

"I wonder if I might have a word with Mr Abbot?"

"Not easy, mate. He's a very busy man. Could you give me an idea of your business?"

"No. Would you just tell him that Superintendent Sutcliffe would like a word with him?"

"Oh. Oh, I see. Right. Won't be a tick."

He bustled back, less cockily, into the house, and was succeeded after a further wait by a very different figure. Walter Abbot was not tall, but he was square and enormously powerful, giving the impression of a rugby player gone to seed. He was brown-suited and bristling with energy that seemed likely to spill over into aggression at any moment—the sort of man whose natural arena would seem to be the boxing ring or the American football field. Not a man to work for, or to live with. Forewarned that his visitor was a policeman, there was a patina of geniality over his aggression, but it was the fleeting geniality of the pugnacious, not the geniality of the genial.

"Well, well, Superintendent. What can I do for you? You'll excuse my not inviting you in, but we *are* very busy today. Just a matter of routine, is it?"

"Not quite routine, sir. I'm investigating the death of Mr James Partridge."

The man's bushy eyebrows raised themselves.

"Really? Funny, I thought everyone agreed that was suicide."

"The inquest returned an open verdict, in fact. Why did you assume it was suicide?"

"Thought they were just being tactful. The rumour around these parts is that the marriage wasn't going too well. She hadn't been up here much of late, his lady. Fine figure of a woman, but a handful, I'd guess. Wouldn't have thought he was much of a dab with the whip hand, the late Mr Partridge. But it was a sad business altogether. He was a fine MP."

"You thought so, did you?"

"Yes, indeed. I'm a member of the local Association—was on the committee that short-listed him for the seat, as a matter of fact. That would be—what?—

five, six years ago, just before the 'seventy-nine election. We thought he'd go far—high office and all that. Didn't quite make it, but a fine man all the same."

"So you didn't have any disagreements with him, later on?"

The eyes narrowed, and a rasp entered the voice.

"No. I've said I thought he was a fine MP. Has some sillyarse been talking?"

"Not so much that, Mr Abbot. But I found your letter yesterday when I went to his cottage."

The man's face was an open playground of emotions. He must certainly be quite unused to hiding them, which surely meant that life was sticky for his workers. Clearly he would have liked to bawl Sutcliffe out for snooping. On the other hand, he was a policeman, and quite possibly he had a warrant or Mrs Partridge's permission. For the moment prudence was victorious in this man of sudden rages and perpetual ill-will.

"Oh, that. Just a little local difficulty. That blew over in no time. We smoothed it over before he died."

"Really? When would that be?"

"Oh, he wrote me a conciliatory reply, and I accepted his apologies by phoning him. We ended the best of friends."

"You couldn't show me his reply?"

" 'Course I couldn't. I wouldn't keep things like that."

"I would have thought you *would*—any business would keep correspondence with an MP. In any case, Mr Abbot, I have a copy of his reply. And it was not conciliatory."

"God damn it!" shouted Abbot, banging his fist down on the gatepost. "If you had a copy of his reply why didn't you say so?"

"To spare you the need of a lie? Why should I? Look, I've got some idea of what this business is all about. Why don't you give me your side of it?"

Abbot looked hard at him, then with an effort brought himself down below boiling point. Sutcliffe had half hoped to be invited into the "farmhouse," but Abbot showed no inclination to do that. Instead he continued leaning on the gate, a massive and intimidating presence.

"I tell you, the man was a busybody and an ignoramus. As you'll know if you've seen the letters, he got a bee in his bonnet about factory farming. I needn't spell it out to you: you'll know the general line these cranks take. 'Will you tell your constituents how much meat will go up by?' I asked him, when I heard about this damned bill of his. It was sheer do-goodery, and ignorant into the bargain. Got it into his head that our animals are mistreated—"

"And are they not?"

"Don't be daft. It's like a four-star hotel in there. Anyone can inspect our premises, and I defy them to find a suffering animal." Since he made no effort to shift his bulk from the gate, Sutcliffe realized his words did not constitute an invitation. "No, it was starry-eyed nonsense. I ask you: would it make sense? Any fool can see it wouldn't be in our interests to mistreat them."

"Isn't that the sort of thing Southern slave-owners used to say?" asked Sutcliffe. The man flashed brick-red and seemed about to explode, so Sutcliffe went on hurriedly: "But I'm not primarily interested in your

farm. I'm interested in your quarrel with Jim Partridge.
When did you first write to him?"

"When I heard about this bill. A load of sentimental
twaddle *that* was. I hear it's stone dead now—"

"Quite. Like James Partridge."

"Yes, well . . . Sorry. Unfortunate turn of phrase.
Well, I wrote to him when I first got wind of what you
might call the general tendency of this bill. Brought a
few facts to his attention."

"And he replied?"

"Yes, he did. Impertinent bloody piece of work.
Acknowledged the truth of some of what I said, but . . .
well, talking a lot of rot about the unnaturalness of the
life. Bloody fool. I wouldn't call an MP's life natural,
but that doesn't mean I want to abolish Parliament!"

"And that was when you wrote that rather intemperate letter that I saw?"

"Intemperate! You call that intemperate? When the
man is threatening my livelihood!"

"And after you received his reply, there was no more
communication between you?"

"No, there wasn't. There was only a week or two,
and then he was dead."

"You never went to his cottage?"

"What would be the point? That time he wrote to
me was the last weekend he was up here."

But Sutcliffe had noted the shadow of equivocation
cross his eyes.

"You haven't answered my question."

"No. I never went there. Only been there once in
my life."

"And you didn't go *after* his death?"

"No, I did not. Now, if you've quite finished—"

"Can I be quite specific? You didn't go to his cottage late one night and try to break in?"

"No. No. No. Get me? No!"

The man bellowed like a bull, the most naturally animal thing in his entire farm.

"Well, well. I'll be saying goodbye for the present. But I might well be back."

"I can't think of any good reason why you should be. Just what sort of an investigation is it you're conducting, Superintendent?"

"It's a very vague, fluid sort of investigation at the moment, sir. But you might say it has murder at the back of its mind."

The man looked at him, curiosity, cunning and apprehension battling it out across his red, porcine face. Then he turned and stumped back into the administrative office. Sutcliffe felt he would not like to be one of his underlings there for the rest of the day.

As luck would have it, the visit was to have a follow-up, and from one of the underlings Sutcliffe had pitied in his heart. That evening, after he had eaten an execrable meal of boiled greens, mashed potato and supermarket meat pie, and while he was washing it down with a glass of tolerable beer in the bar and listening to the assembled hacks swapping the day's campaign gossip, the landlord came in from the back.

"Here, are you a policeman?"

"That's right."

"There's someone on the phone for you, then. You can take it through there in the passage."

Sutcliffe was mystified, and when he found the dingy little nook with the phone said a very cautious "Hello?"

"Are you the policeman that was out at Manor Court

Farm today?" asked a male voice with a rural Yorkshire accent. "Investigating the murder of the MP?"

"The *death* of the MP. Yes, that's right. How did you know I was here?

"To tell you the truth, I had a pint or two myself in the Happy Dalesman last night, and when I looked out the window this morning, I thought I recognized you. Abbot was swearing up hill and down dale when he came in from talking to you, going on about the police, so it wasn't difficult to put two and two together. The thing is, I wondered if he'd told you the whole truth."

"I should think it's very unlikely. Are you willing to fill me in a little?"

"Well now; no names, no pack drill, and then I might. But I don't want any fall-out from what I'm going to tell you. Manor Court Farm is about the only employer that there is in Cordingate, so they've got us all in a cleft stick there. So, I'm not going to give you my name—"

"And I'm in no position to get it, over the telephone."

"Right. Well, this thing goes back well before this bill that Partridge was bringing in. In fact, I'm not sure the bill didn't spring from this visit he made—well before the last election it was, when Partridge was still a minister for something or other—was it Health?"

"He was an under-secretary in the Ministry, yes."

"Right. Well, he came to the farm to see Abbot on some constituency business, Abbot being a big shot with the local Conservative Association, as you probably know. Trouble was, this Friday he came along at five o'clock, just as all of us were streaming out of the place. Now, one of us said that Mr Abbot was still at

work, and Mr Partridge just strolled in, and nobody
liked to stop him, though it was strictly against house
rules. Well, unfortunately Mr Abbot had gone along
to the lavatory: he spends a fair time on the lavatory
seat does Mr Abbot, him being a heavy eater, a heavy
drinker and a heavy anything you'd care to name. So
after he'd waited around for a few minutes, Partridge
goes out to the farm proper, to see if Abbot was down
in any of the sheds."

"And he wandered round and didn't like what he
saw?"

"Dead right he didn't. Chickens with . . . Well, I'll
not go into it. We none of us like it, that work there.
But it's work, isn't it? And these days, in Yorkshire,
you cling for dear life to any job that's going. So he
sees . . . all these things—"

"Isn't the place ever inspected, by the way?"

"Yes, it is. But not very frequently, and Walter Abbot manages to hear of it well in advance. Everything
well above the acceptability threshold when the Ministry of Agriculture people come, I can assure you,
though it is well below it all the rest of the time. Then
it's profit first, profit last, and profit all stations in
between for Walter Abbot. Anyway, there was no row
at the time; Mr Partridge was just thoughtful, so Abbot
told someone. There was a row for us next day, about
letting him in: Abbot charged around the offices bel-
lowing from morning till night, until finally someone
could stand it no more and handed in his notice. Abbot
assumed he'd let Partridge in, and that cooled him down
a bit. But then he heard that Partridge wasn't letting
the matter rest there."

"What was he doing?"

"I don't know in detail. You'd have to ask his politician pals about that. But I do know he was stirring things up in Whitehall, at the Ministry of Agriculture, and so on, about factory farming generally, and us in particular. There was an unscheduled inspection, but of course after his visit there'd been a brisk clean-up around the place: some animals slaughtered, some put out of sight—it's easy enough to do. He's ordered something similar after your visit today. So nothing came of that, but things rumbled on for some time, with Walter Abbot cursing Partridge, and going around chuckling fit to make your blood run cold when he got the boot from the government."

"He couldn't have had anything to do with that, could he?"

"I shouldn't have thought so. He wouldn't have the Prime Minister's ear, would he? If he did, he'd bloody well have told us so, I can tell you. Any road, the next thing we heard was, Partridge had come second in the ballot for Private Members' bills, and was bringing in this so-called Animals' Charter. That was when the correspondence started to fly, and Walter Abbot really began to put the boot in."

"I've read the correspondence. What else did he do?"

"In detail I don't know, because we only heard of it by rumour, or from what he cares to tell anybody when he's in a good humour, which means he's halfway drunk. I know he tried to nobble other members of the Conservative Association to get a vote of no confidence, or something of that sort, with the aim of getting rid of him as the member for Bootham. One or two of them probably played along with him, but I shouldn't think he got very far. It's not a very Conservative thing to do, and besides Walter Abbot isn't a popular personality—not the sort of man most people would want to get too closely associated with. That tinpot führer approach puts most people off. But still, he was certainly going all out to get James Partridge, and Walter Abbot going all out is a fearsome spectacle."

"You don't know if he made any attempt to rob Partridge's cottage after his death? To get his letters back, for example?"

"Don't know anything about that. He could easily have bullied some of the outdoor farmhands to go along with him, if necessary."

"You're probably right. Well, this has been most useful. Is there anything else?"

"Not that I can think of at the moment."

"Tell me, Mr—sir, what exactly is your part in all this? What motive do you have for telling me what you have done?"

"If you'd ever worked for Abbot you wouldn't need to ask. He's the human dregs. But there is one more thing . . . When we heard about this Animals' Charter, one or two people up at the Farm got on to Partridge, very much in the way I'm doing with you now. We gave him information, discussed the sort of things the bill needed to guard against. He was always very courteous, very grateful, and seemed a nice bloke. Now he's gone, and apparently his bill with it. I'd like to see whoever it was did it get caught."

"I wish I could be more confident that you will. But I'll do my best. I'll certainly do my best."

9

Campaigning (II)

Nominations of candidates in the by-election at Bootham East closed on February 17th, and by evening it was clear what an array of political talent the voters of that constituency were to be offered on voting day. The three main parties' candidates were already known, and had been canvassing for more than a fortnight. There were other nationally organized parties, more or less respectable, fielding hopefuls: the Communist Party decided that really they *ought* to show the red flag in depressed, industrial Bootham, though they knew they would have done infinitely better in, say, Hampstead; the National Front (which made token gestures towards respectability, rather as Charles II might appear on state occasions with his queen) thought the constituency was ripe for what they called radical thinking; and the Ecology Party, after much hesitation (for what, after all, had ecology ever done for Bootham?) decided that their ambitions to be a national party as successful as the German Greens obliged them to field a candidate.

And then there were the rest.

Taking them slowly, one by one, they were: the Home Rule for England candidate; the Women for the Bomb candidate; Yelping Lord Crotch, the Top of the Pops candidate; the Transcendental Meditation candidate; the Transvestite Meditation candidate (Ms Humphrey Ward); the John Lennon Lives candidate; The Bring Back Hanging candidate; the Britain Out of the Common Market candidate; the Richard III Was Innocent candidate; and Zachariah ZZugg, the I'm Coming Last candidate.

This mixture of the aspiring, the exhibitionist and the plain dotty made up the choice that would be presented on the ballot papers of Bootham East. This list, to the joy of the nation, though decreasingly so, had by tradition to be read out every time the nation's television or radio broadcast coverage of the by-election. Shortly afterwards the government was to increase the amount demanded as deposit by electoral hopefuls, in order to discourage lunatic fringe candidates. The government had a very shaky grasp of psychology.

February 17th had begun quite well for Jerry Snaithe. You wouldn't have thought it was going to be one of those bitch days when all sorts of niggling little things go wrong.

First Susan had come up by the early train. He had gone to meet her, and so had the press photographer from the *Mirror* to whom he had casually mentioned the time of her arrival the day before. They were photographed kissing on the platform, and though Sue had grimaced in distaste, Jerry was delighted.

"You're the only wife in this campaign," he told Sue. "Except for the loonies—I expect some of them have wives."

"Thanks very much." said Sue.

It was, for February, a lovely day. When they got to campaign headquarters they found that the ancient central heating in the house (always inclined, like Jerry, to blow hot or cold quite unpredictably) was making the place into a kind of hothouse. The bruiser at the bottom of the stairs, the veteran of innumerable pit-head confrontations with police and scabs, had changed his T-shirt for a string vest, out of which he bulged unpredictably with quite tremendous displays of muscle and belly.

"Who on earth's that?" Sue whispered to Jerry, as they went up the stairs.

"Our bouncer," Jerry whispered back, as if even he were unwilling to take any chances with the gentleman's temper.

"I didn't know you were running a casino here. Are party funds that low?"

"He's to keep the media in their place, that's all."

"Oh Jerry, you are a hypocrite. You know you love the media. Publicity is your life's blood."

"I enjoy *using* the media. I don't *love* them," explained Jerry, as if to a backward child.

The press conference started well, too. They had a bald-headed member of the Shadow Cabinet, who said supportive things in a reassuringly moderate way. Sue sat on the platform with Jerry and the rest, and said a few words about her work in Hackney, and the hideous effects of government cuts on underprivileged families.

She did well, because she knew her facts and kept it simple. Jerry thought to himself that he'd have to put pressure on her to up her contribution to the campaign. The morning's conference was nearly over when the little pot-bellied man from the *Daily Grub* got up.

"Could Mr Snaithe tell us where he went to school?"

"I went to school in Yorkshire," said Jerry, a shade too quickly. "It's in the campaign biography."

"Quite," said the *Grub* man. "We've all done our homework. I wanted to know which school it was you went to."

There was one thing you had to say for Jerry, his opponents (and they were legion) always admitted: he was very good at damage-limitation. He knew at once when he had to come clean. He put on a sort of self-deprecating smile—a smile that would have had some old ladies eating out of his hand, and other, sharper ones itching to run him through with their umbrellas.

"I went to Amplehurst. It's a Roman Catholic school, to the north of here. My people—my parents were Roman Catholic. You could say I had a privileged education. It's *because* I had a privileged education that I'm against elitist education in all shapes and forms, and the obscenity of people buying privilege for their kids."

The *Grub* man smiled happily, pleased at having made his point.

"I always wondered why you used 'media' as a plural," he said, sitting down. "Shows what a classical public school education does for you."

"Surprised anyone from the *Grub* would notice," said Jerry. He said it genially, and the audience laughed.

It was cleverly done. Sue had to admire him for it. Or admire it in him. Jerry himself sat back, moderately content. He had fielded that well. If it had to come out, that was the best line to take. Jerry had long ago forgotten that he had in fact very much enjoyed his schooldays, which had suited his inclination to believe in the survival of the fittest. Jerry at that time had been very fit.

When the press conference was over, they all went back to headquarters to prepare for a morning's canvassing, and the reporters milled around too, collecting their copies of the morning's handouts. It was while they were milling around at the bottom of the stairs, and while the bruiser was examining closely the credentials of one of the political staff of *The Times* (he peered close and long at it, whether because his eyesight had been impaired by long years at the coal face, or because he'd never learnt to read with any confidence, nobody would have dared ask him), that the political correspondent of the *Daily Strip* noticed something interesting. The bruiser's new, or rather *not* new, string vest showed up with hideous clarity the tattoos which undulated their way up his brawny arms and around his bull neck and throat: snakes entring through the legs of one naked woman after another, all the women busty and welcoming, adorned with names like FANNY and MANDY and uttering invitations like COME AND GET ME and I'M RIPE, RANDY, AND READY, and the reporter (conscious of the editorial decision that the political content of the *Daily Strip* should never be more than three per cent of the whole) was wondering whether something of a general and salacious interest might be made of these, when he saw, under the horrendously detailed and lifelike pair of snakes that curled their way around the man's neck, a slogan previously hidden by the back of his T-shirt: I'M WHITE. The *Strip* man smiled to himself and got out his notebook.

Jerry and Sue and the visiting Shadow Cabinet man had a very successful morning's canvass. They were doing door-to-door in the part of Somertown that lay in his constituency (which in fact had very nearly been called Bootham Somertown—if it had been, it would have been the most misleadingly titled constituency since Sheffield Brightside). Jerry throve on the poverty, the neglect, the filthy toddlers, the debris that littered the front gardens, the peeling paintwork and the matted, dead weeds. In the streets the young men, idle, were hunched over clapped-out cars like priests tinkering with the souls of dying sinners. In kitchens radios and cassette-recorders blared and babies howled. Susan was wonderful, Jerry had to admit it. She knew areas like this, people like this; she knew how to talk to them. So did he, in a way, expert and experienced canvasser that he was, but he wondered if he was quite as good at listening. So he let Sue listen, and then gave them a bit of uplift at the end about getting to the polling stations. They all responded to him warmly. In spite of my public school education, he told himself with a satisfied smile.

At lunch-time the canvassing party and the hangers-on all stopped at a pub for beer and sandwiches. In some parts of the constituency you could do this, in other parts it wasn't wise. In Somertown you definitely could do it. Jerry praised Sue's morning's work to the skies, and thanked her sincerely. Why does he make me feel like just another constituency worker? Sue wondered. Then Jerry told her she could take the afternoon off.

"Why?"

"We're having a march through town with Albert Scadgett, the sheet-metalworkers' leader."

"I can come along. I have the use of my legs."

"No, no. You represent a different side to my image. We don't want to get the ideas mixed up. The Shadow Cabinet man is sloping off too, though that's because he wouldn't be seen dead with Albert. You go and do some shopping."

Sue's eyebrows raised themselves, delicately dangerous.

"I'm sure I shall find lots of things to buy in Bootham that I couldn't get in London."

"Well, there's blood puddings," said Jerry, humourously, but not registering the danger. His attention, in any case, was diverted by the reporter from the *Daily Strip*, who had been following them around with unusual devotion throughout the canvass.

"Mr Snaithe?"

"Yes?"

"Are you employing Fascist thugs in your campaign?"

Jerry gave a tired, seen-it-all smile.

"Fascist thugs? Is this another media scare? Do you really imagine I'm likely to employ Fascists? You know my record. There's been no more dedicated anti-Fascist on the GLC than me—"

"Do you realize that the bully-boy that you employ at your HQ to keep us at bay has I'M WHITE tattooed on the back of his neck?"

Jerry smiled, pityingly.

"You're libelling a dedicated Socialist—and one put out of work by the policies of this government. I suppose it never occurred to you, did it, that his name was White? Syd White?"

"Here," said Jerry Snaithe to his agent, as the march which he was to lead with Albert Scadgett was assembling on the outskirts of town. "What's the name of our rough-trade kid?"

"Who?"

"Our bully-boy protecting us from the media."

"Reg Bickerstaffe. Why?"

"Get rid of him, eh?"

"If you say so. Any reason?"

"You'll see soon enough, if the media play true to form. Try and replace him with a black, will you?"

"I can try. But the ethnic vote in this constituency's not worth a tinker's cuss. Why a black?"

"They don't tattoo easily," said Jerry.

Oliver Worthing was lost. It had happened rather too often in the last election, and now it had happened in this. After a bit of light canvassing in an area sympathetic to middle-ground politics, they had had half an hour's break before the next item on the day's schedule. Oliver had driven home to see to his cat, which had been out all night. The cat was bedraggled and cheeky, and when he had seen to her needs Oliver had driven off to Gigglesworth Middle School for a question-and-answer session with the seniors. But was it Gigglesworth Middle School he was supposed to be at? he asked himself, as he parked in the staff car park. Or was it Perkdale High? Or even Clunmeadow High? His agent had shouted to him as he drove off: "Remember—it's eleven o'clock at . . ." Where? Gigglesworth, Perkdale or Clunmeadow? All those names were as familiar and everyday to him, a local counselor, as Whitehall or Downing Street were to a Westminster politician. But which of them had actually been named?

It was no good—he would have to go in and ask. To say, in effect, "I am here; am I supposed to be?" was rather humiliating, but the school secretary was sympathetic, and she rang round to the other two and established that where he was supposed to be was Perkdale High. Even the headmaster came in and shook his hand and wished him well. Headmasters were congenitally well-disposed towards middle-ground politics.

Bells had sounded while they were exchanging hurried civilities, and as he made his way back to his car children were changing classrooms amid clatter, laughter and shouts. Pushing his way hurriedly through the surging throngs, he was amused to hear how the by-election was sharpening schoolboy wit. He laughed when he heard one scruffy teenager say to his mate:

"He looks lost. He must be a politician."

The smile left his lips when he heard the mate's reply: "Don't you know him? That's Oliver Worthing. The Borstal boy."

Antony Craybourne-Fisk's day, or so he thought, had begun very nicely indeed. His grandmother had arrived the evening before, and was to spend the morning canvassing and speaking with him. He had lodged her at

the Unicorn, and taken the precaution of moving out
that day to Penny's cottage, in case she was too appalling, or too demanding in the matter of grandfilial
duties. But she turned out to be a spry and forceful old
lady, eminently presentable, with the remains still on
her of a classical loveliness which it would have been
difficult to find any trace of in her grandson. When
Antony picked her up the next morning she said she
had had such an un*u*sual breakfast, served by such a
nice type of young man, a type she had known in her
younger days, but thought had died out. Antony was
not sure of the degree of irony behind these remarks,
and merely replied that he was glad.

She was wearing an enormous, voluminous fur
("Ivor's, darling: I bought it at the sale of his effects")
over a summery frock in yellows and greens that emphasized her queenly, impressive figure. She walked
with difficulty, but with a certain game dignity. Antony
warmed to her, or at least he warmed to himself for
taking the risk of inviting her.

They were first to tour the constituency in the loudspeaker car, concentrating on the better-heeled areas
and the suburbs where the older generation was to be
found in large numbers. This went awfully well: Granny
Masterson's voice rang out through the streets like Vera
Lynne announcing her next number at a troop concert.
Now and again, when there was a little knot of shops,
they got out so that Antony could introduce her to the
shoppers ("Isobel Ainslie, the actress, but to me she's
my Granny Masterson"). She caused a frisson of interest such as Antony on his own never evoked, and
she revelled in her audience.

The morning was to end in the town square, as lunch-time began. They had rigged up their makeshift plat-form there, and Antony had concocted a little speech of which he was proud: after an introductory sentence about the historic opportunity which the by-election presented to the voters of Bootham, he intended to launch off, with a paragraph beginning "I have a vi-sion . . . ," into five minutes of perfumed hot air which he had sweated over the night before. Granny Master-son was to sit on the platform, gazing admiringly, and then finish the proceedings off with a five-minute puff for him. Unfortunately Granny Masterson demurred.

"No, darling: in *this* performance I am merely the warm-up artist. I shall say my little piece first, then ev*ap*orate into the crowd and watch your performance from among the grrroundlings. I know you will be perfectly *splen*did!"

She patted his knee in the back seat of the car, and he smiled at her a smile which she recognized as com-pounded mostly of self-love (for who would more read-ily recognize self-love than a member of the acting profession?).

When they got to the town square there was already a gratifying little knot of people awaiting them, some of them Conservative stalwarts summoned by the party agent, some determined theatre-goers who remembered Isobel Ainslie from those rep days in Sheffield in the 'fifties. They gave her the sort of cheer the English give to a gallant trouper, and she clambered stiffly up on to the platform ("Whoops, darling!") and delicately fin-gered the microphone as if it were the hand of a royal suitor. She gave her all in introducing her grandson, ending up in hortatory voice: "I know you're all going to *run* along to the polling booths, or whatever they call those little places, and give your *ster*ling support on February 27th to Antony, and to the Conservative Party."

She had not paused before "Conservative Party," but she had said it very distinctly, as if it was a line she had had difficulty learning. Then she clambered heavily down off the platform, waving graciously, and went determinedly into the crowd, shaking hands enthusiastically with her fans from long-ago, autographing the odd yellowing programme and flirting outrageously with the men. The middle-aged and elderly of Bootham loved her.

"Oh, Miss Ainslie, I remember you so well in *Private Lives—*."

"Do you, darling? So kind of you. I played it twice, you know. Popular demand. Noel was going to come, but he had to fly back to Jamaica to escape the tax people. *Such* a lovely part!"

"And that American play," said the man, "the one there was all the fuss about."

"My Blanche du Bois! Second only to Vivien's they do say, and a part I always loved. Playwrights don't *write* parts for actresses any more. We're positively a forgotten species."

"I have a vision . . ." the voice of Antony had raised itself to a Joan of Arc fervour from the platform, but it went unheeded.

"And in films, too," said an aged lady. "I remember you before the war in *Nelson's Emma*."

"Yes, darling, and in *The 'Forty-Five*, cavorting with

Bonnie Prince Charlie in the hay, if I'm not mistaken. Small parts, but awfully telling. Dear Alexander Korda. I was quite a protégée of his. I was a starlet when starlets *were* starlets! Don't talk to me about Rank! Pooh!"

"And weren't you one of the nurses in *Green for Danger*?" asked a well-set-up man with a drooping moustache, who was in fact Superintendent Sutcliffe, come to Bootham in the hope of catching James Partridge's agent in one of his odd moments of free time.

"Yes indeed. What a darling film—everyone adored it, and *so* exciting. And then in *Passport to Pimlico*. But I *loved* those years in Sheffield," she went on, not entirely truthfully, for they had hardly signified an advancement in her career. "For any actress worth her salt the *stage* will always be her true home."

"And always the best parts," said one of the men.

"*Always* the star parts. People were so kind . . ."

"And now you've come back up here," said a sentimental lady, "to play a supporting role to your grandson—"

"Who, darling?"

"Your grandson. The Conservative candidate."

"Oh, little pushy! Yes, one has to do one's bit, you know. Children! Always such a problem. Did you ever see my Gertrude? . . ."

Soon Antony's oration (which had not had quite the effect of his namesake's over the body of Caesar) was over, and, pressed by photographers, he had come over to be taken with his grandmother. She posed like a professional, best profile forward, but as Antony and his agent melted away she said loudly "Who was that?" There was a little nervous laughter, and Isobel Ainslie gave one of her wickedest sideways glances. Then she confessed that she was tired.

"Awfully exhausting, doing my all for little whatsis-name. Darlings, I spy my hotel over there, and it has a perfectly charming little bar with a *divine* little Sicilian gigolo who *adores* me, and I wonder if one of you could just give me an arm to lean on—"

Many arms shot out, but Sutcliffe's was the first and the most stalwart. "I'll look after Mrs Masterson," he said, in his most pukka voice. She shot him a brave, grateful smile.

"Thank you . . . So kind . . . A cavalier! What was that line, now? 'I have always depended on the kindness of strangers . . .' "

And, hobbling slowly and painfully, Blanche du Bois exited in the direction of the Unicorn Hotel.

10

Dear Old Granny

They made their way slowly but with a
certain style in the direction of the Trueman Bar of the
Unicorn Hotel. It was a little side bar that did not serve
eats, and now, at nearly two, it was practically deserted.
Only one other couple was seated there, the woman
sipping her glass sceptically.

"No, don't complain: it's quite interesting. I've never
had a gin and soda before."

Gianni was behind the bar.

As Sutcliffe settled Granny Masterson—or Isobel
Ainslie, as he preferred to think of her—down in a
comfortable corner, Gianni smouldered over to them.
He was, Sutcliffe thought, one of the few things in the
industrial desert that was Bootham that was smoul-
dering. Isobel Ainslie appeared delighted to see him.

"Oh, here's Fairy Lightfoot, my own favourite dago!
Ciao, Gianni! Campari soda, darling. I strongly recommend you to have it too. He understands both words,
don't you, Don Giovanni?"

But Sutcliffe, who had once holidayed on Lake Garda, experimented with *"Birra?,"* and actually got just that. The triumph he felt was lessened by the two pounds Gianni gave him as change from a five-pound note.

"Well!" said Isobel Ainslie. "This *is* nice. How lovely to find people who remember me—and so affectionately, too! Glowing memories, wouldn't you say? Of course, they do too in the Home, but there we're all in the Profession. They all crowd around if they show one of my old films on television, but then I have to crowd round when *their* old films are shown. Actually to be remembered by the public! So good for the old ego, darling. I really am glad I decided to come."

"Was it a surprise to be asked?"

"Bolt from the blue, darling. Hadn't heard from him for years, and didn't expect to. Knew he was standing, that was all."

"Why do you think he asked you?"

"Oh, to show off the only Yorkshire connection he has, of course. Quite silly. They all remember me, and come along and get my autograph, but whoever heard of anyone voting for someone because he had a Yorkshire grandmother? I really think, you know, that that young man is underestimating his voters."

Sutcliffe thought again what a sharp old lady Isobel Ainslie was.

"So you hadn't seen your grandson for a while, Mrs—"

"Call me Isobel. As one gets older there are fewer and fewer who do. No, not for *years*, darling. In fact, I can remember the last time. It was on Waterloo Station, or Victoria, or somewhere, and I was on my way

to a television studio somewhere to film an episode of
Steptoe, in which I had a *lovely* little part, and he was
on his way to Stowe or Lancing or whatever school it
was he went to. Old Mrs Craybourne who brought
him up was with him, going to give him a bust-up at
the Savoy, or the Ritz. Anyway, I was in a fearful rush
and I gave him half-a-crown, which he made it dev-
astatingly clear was not enough."

"And that was the last time?"

"The last time. It was a miracle I recognized him
then, because I'd only seen him five or six times. I
think he knew *me*, in fact, from the odd television
appearance. As you see, though I was reasonably ma-
ternal with twerpie's mother, by the time I got to be a
*grand*mother, the instinct was wearing very thin indeed. Perhaps it was just intuition—telling me how he
would turn out."

"So he wasn't brought up by his mother?"

"Good Lord, no. That wasn't Virginia's line at all.
I'd had *her* right at the beginning of my career—1934,
it was, when I was still doing little bits and pieces for
Mr Cochrane."

"You were married?"

"Good heavens, *yes*. One *was* in those days. He was
someone who did things with stocks and shares in the
city—just like little Antony . . . in many respects. Sleek
and ever so slightly crooked. We were married at least
in name until I came to Sheffield, which he said was
the last straw. Anyway, I did my best with Virginia,
but then I began to get small parts in films, and one
had to, well, farm her out, find people to look after
her most of the day. By the time she was in her teens

she was *lovely*—just beautiful, darling—but the teeni-
est bit wild."

"What happened to her?"

"Virginia? . . . *What* an unfortunate choice of name!
. . . Well, when she was seventeen she married, very
hurriedly, Mr Fisk, who was a solicitor in Great Yar-
mouth, of all places. That didn't last, as anyone could
have predicted. There was Antony, but when she bolted
she took him with her."

"Bolted?"

"With Mr Craybourne. He became a Tory MP, and
the marriage lasted five years or more, which was something of a record for Virginia. When she bolted the
second time she didn't take Antony with her . . ."
Meditating, she emitted a fruity chuckle. "Probably a
good thing, really: young puppy out there would probably have a seven-barrelled name instead of a double-
barrelled one by now."

"She changes partners, does she?"

"Worse than a square-dance, darling! Gets passed
from hand to hand. Marvellous really that she can still
do it at her age, though I remember I . . . Ah well.
Nothing worse than the salacious reminiscences of the
elderly, is there?"

"So Antony was brought up by step-parents, was
he?"

"Actually by this Craybourne's *mother*. She was a
silly creature, and she made a bad job of it by the look
of the little creep, but I do think one should be grateful
that she did it at all, don't you? I rather gather he came
to her as a sort of godsend, to give her an interest in
her old age, and certainly it must have been good for

the poor little mite to feel *wanted* by someone. But perhaps she rather overdid it, don't you think? He rather does assume that he is the centre of everybody else's universe, as well as his own. When he asked me to come up, it was definitely as if he were doing a favour to me, rather than the reverse. No, a silly woman, I'm afraid. She suggested he take the double-barrelled name, you know, and in giving him that she seems to have given him a double-barrelled opinion of himself."

"And did he keep contact with his mother?"

"Oh yes, *some*. It was always, frankly, rather difficult to keep *track* of Virginia, let alone contact with her, but she would phone now and then, or descend on the Craybournes for a visit, or take him off for a meal or a pantomime somewhere. She meanwhile went from flower to flower: there was Rotherbrook the newspaper tycoon, there was Lord Prestonpans—she never actually married either of those, so she never got a title, poor duck. There was supposed to be an Arab sheikh, and she *did* marry him, but he turned out to be an Egyptian greengrocer, and I think all her experience of the mysterious Orient took place in the Cromwell Road. There were others—heavens there were others!—and now I believe she's married to some Greek gigolo or other. Talking of which—"

Sutcliffe signalled to Gianni to bring replenishments. As he did so, something caught his eye in the street outside. The Labour Party march through town, headed by Jerry Snaithe and Albert Scadgett, was leaving the town square and threading its way past the Unicorn Hotel. Sutcliffe recognized Jerry Snaithe from his picture in the newspapers, and Albert Scadgett from his

innumerable appearances on television during the sheet
metalworkers' strike of last year. He was a conserva-
tively-dressed man with a prim, rosebud mouth, on
which was planted an expression of the most intense
self-approval. Last year had been his great year: then
he had led the sheet metalworkers to defeat through
month after punishing month, had appeared daily on
the news bulletins, had had missiles hurled at him by
Tory harridans. Then it had been his proud boast to
have brought the soup kitchen back to Yorkshire. Now,
since the strike had collapsed, his fame was on the wane.
Already the other couple in the Trueman Bar were
discussing whether he was a television quiz-show chairman, or the villain in *Emmerdale Farm*. But today was
Albert Scadgett's big chance to relive fleetingly the heady
days of last year's fiasco, and hence that expression of
self-approval that curled his tiny mouth into something
approaching a smile.

"No, darling," Mrs Masterson was saying, over her
second Campari soda, when Sutcliffe brought his attention back to her, "I only had the one, but Virginia
goes through husbands as if they were paper tissues."

"All well-heeled, I suppose?"

"Yes, darling, but *less* so, as she's got older. Of course
it was always her great ambition to get into the aris-
tocracy. I've never understood that, myself. To me
they're overrated. Always wanting something *new* and
outré, which can be tedious as well as physically dangerous. Jaded palates aren't very interesting to the other
party. Anyway, she never *did* get in, though she's certainly frisked around the fringes."

"And what has your grandson done since school?"

"Oh, darling—why ask me? The last few years it's

just been the ring on my birthday between Virginia and
me. *If that.* So I really haven't heard. When I lived in
London I heard a bit more. There *was* some scandal
about forged ballot papers for an election to the Oxford
University Conservative Association. Antony was
standing for President, but the election was disallowed.
Antony said it was some over-enthusiastic supporter
of his, and that this sort of thing happened all the time
in the Oxford Conservative Association anyway, so
nobody took it too seriously . . . I can't really imagine
what an over-enthusiastic supporter of Antony would
look like, can you, darling?"

"Difficult. Was there anything else?"

"Oh—so *long* ago . . . Women—just the odd one
or two, I think, who could be useful to him . . . One
or two little financial coups, but don't ask *me* about
them, because I never did understand my husband's
little coups (probably just as well) and I really know
nothing at all about Antony's. Funny how he's taken
after Masterson, isn't it? Perhaps that's why I've taken
against him . . . I do know he has a very good friend
who's MP for Crawley or some such place (I remember
the name because it seemed somehow appropriate), and
they've been in one or two 'good things' together . . ."

She had been talking away, propelled along by Sutcliffe's discreet questioning. Now she pulled herself up,
as if she didn't quite know how it had happened.

"But darling—what am I talking about my daughter
and my grandson for, to a *fan*? Naturally you want to
talk about me!"

Sutcliffe had become very fond of Isobel Ainslie, and
he let her talk about "*me*" for quite a time, during

which the old lady bought two rounds of drinks, and determinedly paid Gianni at roughly 1964 prices. When Sutcliffe emerged again into the street (having seen her to her bedroom and left her to have her "afternoon zizz"), he realized that it was already half past three. Bootham in mid-afternoon was displaying no signs of election fever: it was merely being its listless and depressing self. Sutcliffe did see Albert Scadgett, wandering around rather disconsolately, as if his moment of glory had been much briefer than he had expected, as indeed had been the case. He had, when the march ended, volunteered enthusiastically for anything that Jerry or his Campaign Manager would care to give him to do, but he had been given the same casual brush-off by Jerry that Sue had got earlier in the day. Albert Scadgett had served his turn: he had come, he had said nothing (just five words from Albert Scadgett could mean hundreds of lost votes), but Jerry had been seen with him, to the delight of his militant supporters. Now he could be dropped—and Jerry dropped him. Won't somebody recognize me? Albert Scadgett seemed to be saying, as he wandered listlessly around. Perhaps even ask for my autograph?

Sutcliffe made several attempts to phone Bootham Conservative Headquarters, and when he finally got through, *another* young lady with a Roedean accent (not very wise, surely, in Bootham?) informed him that the Tory Agent was fan*tas*tically busy as he could imagine, and really an interview was *quite* out of the question . . . Unless, perhaps, he was from the Press?

"Not the Press, the Police," said Sutcliffe.

"Ah—oh yes—ah well . . ." It was clearly a matter

of comment at Tory Campaign Headquarters that investigation was still continuing into the death of Bootham's former member. The girl was uncertain what to do, or what tone of voice to adopt. Finally, and in chilling tones, the girl said that she could *squeeze* him in for ten minutes tomorrow at three-fifteen.

"I might need fifteen minutes," said Sutcliffe.

"That you will have to arrange with Mr Fawcett," said Roedean, severely.

So Sutcliffe, in watery, late-afternoon sun, went and did what he had intended to do for some days: pay his respects to the local police. The Bootham superintendent was pleasant and cooperative, but Sutcliffe refrained from telling him that from tomorrow he was officially on holiday. The man was interested in the case, because he had actually met James Partridge, on more than one occasion.

"Intelligent man. I liked him. Interested and sympathetic—to the police, I mean—without being uncritically fulsome, in that way Tory politicians have. He understood at once the real problem of police work."

"Boredom?"

"Aye. There's not many grasp that. He was a quiet type (not many politicians like *that*, in my experience) but you felt he was completely dependable."

"Ever meet his wife?"

"Aye."

"Impression?"

"Bitch."

"Got it in five letters. Want to do something that would have pleased Partridge if he were still alive?"

"I'd be happy to, if I can."

"Know a man called Walter Abbot?"

"I *do*."

"Got anything on him?"

"Not anything like what I ought to have on him, I suspect. One drunken driving conviction, three years ago. Gets himself driven around by his underlings these days. Makes a great noise around town, that one—a blow-hard and a bully. Still, he's not one we can cross without good reason."

"Could you organize a spot-check on his so-called farm—by your men, who would then submit a detailed report to the Ministry of Agriculture? There've been Ministry inspections, but the man has obviously got inside contacts, so none of them have been worth the paper they're written on. I'd like to see a real report on the state of the place—and I know James Partridge would have done too."

"It could be done, I suppose. But is it worth it? Has it got anything to do with the man's death?"

"I've no idea. But it has a lot to do with his life— what he had been giving his time to in the last few months before he died. Will you do it?"

"Surely. What you've got in mind is some sort of tribute to his memory, is it?"

"Right. But take your time. I hear my visit has made him nervy. Leave it for four or five weeks, till after the election. Then go in and get him."

11

Party Agent

"You did me a good turn with that suggestion," said the *Grub* man to Sutcliffe that night in the Saloon Bar.

"Suggestion?"

"About Snaithe's schooldays. I've been following it up, and they're making a spread of it in tomorrow's paper."

"What was he? The rabble-rouser against clerical tyranny? The Robespierre of the Fourth Form Revolution?"

"Not at all. Quite the reverse, and it makes an even better story, from our point of view. I'm glad I made the trip there. It was all quite interesting."

And so it had been. *Grub* had driven over to Amplehurst, having first ascertained that it was a Catholic Public School run by members of the Benedictine order. This information conveyed little to him, beyond some associations with a liqueur, but he sat in his car in the centre of the little village of Amplehurst, and

waited until he caught sight of a tall, elderly gentleman
in a billowing habit. Rightly judging this to be one of
the adherents of St Benedict, he followed him into the
village store, where he was purchasing tobacco (the
founder of the order, whose rule Chaucer's Monk had
found over-strict, had presumably not foreseen the in-
vention of tobacco), and there he struck up a conversation with him. Then he had walked back with him
—a leisurely, chatty walk—to the gates of the school
itself. The conversation had ranged over a variety of
subjects, for *Grub* was under no illusion that the monk,
courteously chatty though he was, would talk know-
ingly about ex-pupils to a member of the Press. But
eventually they had got on to the subject of Jerry Snaithe.

"Jeremy Grayling-Snaithe, as he was always called
then," the monk had explained in his tired, cultivated
voice. "The Grayling-Snaithes are rather a good family.
A good *Catholic* family, I mean. Came over in the
1850s. Father was in the Diplomatic, posted here there
and everywhere, seldom appearing for parents' day or
things like that. The boy was very keen then—committed Catholic, keen on keeping the other boys up
to the mark. In fact, he was terribly committed all
round—very sporty, captain of the first fifteen, very
useful cricketer, in the school swimming team. Came
down very hard on slackers and on the arty types. Very
keen on the OTC, and kept all the younger boys up
to scratch. I had an idea that he joined the army later,
after university, but I may be wrong. I only teach the
lower forms, you see. Certainly we never thought of
him as a rabble-rouser—quite the reverse. He was a
natural leader—the only thing was that one wasn't quite

sure of his judgment of *where* he should be leading people."

"It was all marvellously usable stuff," said *Grub*, concluding his pint of beer and his report to Sutcliffe. "I walked two miles there and back and I haven't done *that* since National Service days. But it was well worth it. It'll make a first-rate story."

"Interesting," said Sutcliffe. "A case of the leopard rearranging his spots rather than changing them, wouldn't you say? Fascinating that while Antony Craybourne-Fisk has acquired his double-barrel, Jeremy Grayling-Snaithe has jettisoned his."

"That's it. Happens all the time. Antony Wedgwood Benn becomes Tony Benn and hopes that everyone will forget all about the Wedgwoods—though he remembered that Grandfather Wedgwood used to hunt around Chesterfield when he wanted to get the Chesterfield seat."

"And somehow all this committed Catholic and officer-class stuff got transmuted into committed Socialism and class-warrior stuff. Interesting. One wonders how it happened."

"Doesn't one ever! There's potential for all sorts of digging there. That sort of thing happened regularly enough in the 'sixties, but this would have happened very late in the radical boom at the earliest, and probably well after it. *Was* he in the army? I wonder. Still, I mustn't go on about it. I suppose you're not really interested in this by-election."

It was common knowledge, since he had received the phone call from the Manor Court Farm worker, that he was a police officer, and that he was nosing into the

Partridge death. If Sutcliffe had not been so cagey, and if their newspapers had not been Tory to a rag, the various reporters would have made something of this by now, and still might. Sutcliffe kept his cage tightly locked.

"Oh, I don't know," he said.

"Here—you did me a good turn, and I'll do you one in exchange. What I'd suggest to you is: the election you should be interested in is not this one, but the last one."

"Oh?"

"That's it. Stands to reason, if you think about it. From your point of view the interesting election is the General Election of 1983. See, this Tory chap and the Labour chap are just Johnny-come-latelies: they couldn't have placed Bootham on the map, I bet you, before this constituency became vacant. That's why they have to dredge up their Yorkshire grandmothers and their Yorkshire schooldays, and so on. And of course none of the loonies was around then, because a General Election doesn't bring you in the same publicity. What does that leave us with? The only person who's actually fought Jim Partridge in an election is Mr Oliver Worthing."

"And?"

"*And* there was a funny rumour going around at the last election that's beginning to surface again this time. And that is that Mr Oliver Worthing's education was even more interesting than Jerry Snaithe's. The rumour goes that he spent part of it in Borstal, and that for a pretty serious offence."

"Really?"

"Might be worth looking into, eh? Now, don't say I never return a favour. And if there's a story in it, keep it for me, eh?"

The story of Jerry Snaithe's education certainly made a good splash in the *Grub* on the next morning. But perhaps even better was the story of Jerry's bruiser in the *Strip* of the same day. Neither the *Grub* nor the *Strip* was in any real sense a newspaper. They were the successors to the weekend strip-and-sensation sheets that Sutcliffe had read and gained his knowledge of the female anatomy from in his boyhood, the only difference being that the *Grub* and the *Strip* catered for the same tastes daily. If anything, the *Strip* was one degree more moronic than the *Grub*, and the paper really went to town on Reg Bickerstaffe, the Labour Party's bouncer. After he had been paid off by the Labour agent, he had been followed by the *Strip* reporter from campaign headquarters and into a pub, where the reporter had bought him many a pint of ale, and had encouraged him, by his human sympathy, to talk not only about his unjust sacking, but also about his political beliefs. These last were perhaps not coherent enough to justify their being called a philosophy, but with judicious prompting from *Strip* Reg Bickerstaffe enlarged at length on the feelings he had towards Pakis, wogs, Yids, nig-nogs, black-arse bastards and so on—interspersed with his views on bints, tarts, and various unprintable synonyms for woman, whom he regarded with blanket and uniform contempt. It made a wonderful story for the *Strip*, the more so as the paper could print the racist and sexist terms, or at least a judicious selection of them, and then hold up its hands virtuously in horror and ask: are these the sort of attitudes that the Labour Party in Bootham upholds? It had it both ways in no uncertain fashion, and the picture of the bouncer's right arm and chest and belly were among the most fascinatingly off-putting that the paper had run for years.

Certainly, Sutcliffe thought, as he ploughed through the populars, it wasn't Jerry Snaithe's day.

He had a late lunch in a Bootham pub that offered fare a notch or two above that of the Happy Dalesman. Then he decided to walk to the Tory campaign headquarters. As he approached them up Gordon Street he picked the place out at once, from the frenetic activity that was going on inside and outside the house. But as he neared it, in a leisurely fashion, a little cavalcade of vehicles drove off, one of them bearing Antony Craybourne-Fisk on his way to repel the voters of some part of the constituency or other. So that when Sutcliffe got to the headquarters' outer office, things were comparatively quiet. In one corner a woman with a hat like a dead hedgehog was addressing envelopes, while at a desk, surrounded by telephones, sat a smart, large and intimidating girl. Obviously Roedean. Probably, like Jerry Snaithe, she had been captain of rugby when she was at school.

"Yes?"

"Superintendent Sutcliffe."

"Oh yes . . . Yes . . . Well, Mr Fawcett has said he *may* be able to give you the fifteen minutes." (Certainly a sense of humour was not one of this girl's strong points. She should, on past form, go far in the party.) "But please remember how busy he is. Through there."

She pointed to a door, and Sutcliffe obediently knocked

on it and entered. Harold Fawcett was on the phone, but he cut short the call and came over to shake Sutcliffe by the hand. A comfortable, paunched, cheery type of man—not too bright, perhaps, but reasonably honest if not pushed into a corner.

"Superintendent? Do sit down. Sorry I'm a bit rushed, but you know how it is in a by-election, or if you don't I hope you never find out! It's pandemonium here much of the time, you know. Do you know what they're calling us? The political focal point of the nation."

"The cynosure," agreed Sutcliffe.

"Aye. I meant to look that one up. It's a daunting thought."

"Right, sir, then I'll come straight to the point and save you time," said Sutcliffe, thinking Fawcett displayed some inclination to time-wasting. "You know what I'm here about."

"Aye," agreed Harold Fawcett carefully.

"I want to ask a few random questions, about things that have come up in the course of my little investigation. Could you tell me anything, for example, about Mr Walter Abbot?"

"Ah—Mr Abbot. Well, I'd have to watch my step there. He used to be on our Executive Committee, and he's still what you might call 'prominent in Conservative circles.' He's not a man one would cross lightly. What exactly is it you'd like to know?"

"About his quarrel with James Partridge. I know all about the causes, and the letters that went back and forth, but what exactly did Abbot *do* when things blew up?"

"Well, it was all rather unpleasant, actually. He seemed

to regard this 'Animals Charter' as some sort of personal insult. And once he'd fired off several salvoes through the post he started charging round the constituency trying to stir up people against Partridge."

"What exactly was he trying to do?"

"I don't think he knew himself, exactly. He is a political ignoramus, really. We don't have de-selection in our party, and with the Labour Party pulling itself to pieces with one de-selection after another, the last thing we'd want is for them to be able to point to anything similar happening in our party. I think what he was hoping for was some sort of vote of no confidence, which he thought might make Partridge stand down before the next election, or even resign his seat at once. It was all nonsense."

"He didn't get anywhere?"

"Of course not. He just huffed and puffed, perhaps got one or two individuals on his side, but in the end he put up more backs than Jim Partridge ever could."

"So he'd have known by early December that he wasn't getting anywhere?"

"Oh yes. But, Superintendent—"

"I'm not implying anything. Merely asking. Did you know anything about Partridge's marital affairs up here?"

"Know anything—no. Suspect—? Well, it had been noticed that Mrs Partridge had hardly been in the constituency over the last three or four months before he died. That sort of thing gets itself commented on in Conservative circles. The member's lady is an important person."

"Mrs Partridge was popular?"

"No. But she was the member's wife."

"She seems to have been disappointed and surprised when her husband was dropped from the government. Were you?"

"Surprised, yes. We'd rather been under the impression that he was one of the coming men. We weren't really disappointed, because a back-bencher who does his job is often a better member from the constituency's point of view than a member of the government. And Partridge would certainly have done his job."

"Why do you think he was dropped from the government?"

"That you'd have to ask the Prime Minister."

"I don't think I'm likely to be given the opportunity. I thought you might have heard some rumours."

"Aye, well, I suppose I did. Don't know how reliable they were. What one or two people were saying at the time was—well, it was two things, really. You know he was one of the juniors at Health? Yes, well, he was very much involved in those disputes over nurses' pay, and the pay of people lower down in the Health Service. Now, James was all for efficiency and keeping pay settlements down, but there were people said he actually became convinced that the nurses especially had an unanswerable case."

"Convinced by their arguments?"

"Yes. It was most unfortunate. He went around saying that the State had been capitalizing for years on their dedication. He was very unconvincing when answering parliamentary questions on the subject, because he really felt they'd been hard done by, and he would have liked to right it. Then there was the other thing . . ."

"Yes?"

"Well, I think it goes back to the Abbot business we've been talking about. He started straying outside his own territory. That's not done in politics these days. You keep your nose down to your own particular grindstone. But he started bombarding the Ministry of Agriculture with questions about intensive farming, doing it more or less privately, as government members have to. He used to buttonhole the minister in the Commons bar, have the juniors round to dinner and press them with questions. It was this bee in his bonnet about there being cruelty involved, but taking it up in that way really wasn't done, and people resented it. Now, in both these things there were questions of loyalty involved. Even in cabinet the PM doesn't much like discussion. The relevant minister has his say, the PM backs him up, because they've thrashed it out in advance, and then the rest say 'Yes.' They're not exactly a rubber stamp—"

"No?"

"No, no. But they're certainly not a debating society. So there was a bit of a question-mark against his loyalty, his total commitment. And added to this there was the slight feeling that he was putting his conscience above his loyalty, and that that conscience was being paraded. There's nothing the PM likes less. We've all got consciences, nobody more so, but we don't parade them, that's the line these days. So all this agonizing about animals really went against the grain, and against the whole government image that's been built up. After all, the little buggers don't have a vote!"

"I see. That's all very interesting. Look, I think I've

got two or three minutes of your time left. Could I ask
you about Oliver Worthing?"

"Worthing?" Harold Fawcett perceptibly brightened
up, as the discussion moved outside Tory circles. "I'm
hardly the expert on the opposition."

"Specifically about rumours that surfaced during the
last general election."

"Oh yes: those. Well, I wouldn't say they surfaced.
After all, they never got into the Press."

"But people were talking about them?"

"Well, they were for a bit. We didn't try to make
anything of it, I can assure you."

"How did the rumours get about, then?"

"Well, to tell you the truth, I think it was one of
our members started them. Man called Peterson, came
from Rotherham—that's Oliver Worthing's home town.
He came up with this story that he'd done a term in
Borstal for aggravated assault—don't know how much
there is in it. Didn't check, because we wouldn't have
used it. He suggested we did, but it wasn't our style
at all. Wouldn't touch it."

"But the rumour got around?"

"The Labour people may have spread it. Or this
Peterson may have talked. We've no control over our
members talking, you know. But as a constituency party
we had nothing to do with it, and that I *can* assure
you."

"I see. Still, Worthing may have thought you had."

"Could be. But he's the man to ask."

"Right. Well, I think that's about all." He stood up,
and as he was about to go through the door, he turned:
"Did you actually like James Partridge, Mr Fawcett?"

"Yes. Yes, I think I can say I did. I didn't *know* him, I don't think many did, but what I saw I liked. And I'll tell you one thing: there wasn't a straighter man in politics. I suppose you might say 'faint praise' to that! It's true there aren't many even comparatively straight men in politics, but he was absolutely straight . . . Always, in everything, he did what he thought was right. Not expedient, but right . . . I'll tell you another thing, strictly under your hat and off the record: I'd give fifty of young jackanapes out there for one James Partridge."

He jerked his thumb out in the direction of the twilit constituency, and Sutcliffe had no doubt that the jackanapes he was referring to was the Tory candidate for the seat of Bootham East. How little, Sutcliffe reflected, that young man had the gift of making himself loved.

12

Meetings

As the third week of February drew to a close, the pace of electioneering hotted up. On the day when Sue Snaithe paid her second visit to Bootham and the Labour Party campaign there was no question of Jerry getting away to meet her. The Leader of the Opposition was due that day, and everyone at Bootham Labour Party HQ was working all out to ensure maximum coverage for the visit—and to make sure that he met no members of the Workers for Revolutionary Action group, who deeply disapproved of him, and were liable to become abusive, or even violent in his presence, which would have been a gift for the greatly despised but assiduously courted media.

It was a busy day for everyone, in fact. The Conservatives were fielding the Foreign Secretary, and the Social Democrats had no fewer than two members of the so-called Gang of Four, and were putting on a great cavalcade-cum-party around town. It was all tremendously exciting, or a bit of a giggle, depending on how you took it, and it was becoming possible for the ordinary citizen of Bootham to believe that he was, indeed, at the epicentre of some political earthquake.

All this presented some logistical problems, especially as the various campaign managers of the main parties could hardly get together to arrange schedules, being rival impresarios. They worked, in fact, through the police, who were around in large numbers to protect the Foreign Secretary from his political opponents, and the Leader of the Opposition from his political supporters. Even then, there was very nearly an Encounter of Opposites. The Leader of the Opposition (a red-haired, smiling man, whom everybody seemed to like, but nobody much wanted to vote for) was in the Merrivale Centre, a shoddy shopping complex, five years old and already looking fifty. He was shaking hands and chatting amiably with shoppers, as if he himself had just dropped in for a packet of pork sausages. Just as his scheduled visit was ending, there appeared at the other end of one of the cavernous, litter-strewn passages the Foreign Secretary (a nervous, retiring man, who now and again gave off very faint whiffs of personality), trying himself to give the impression that he'd just dropped in for a lamb chop. The Labour Leader called cheerily, "Come to sit by the Tory deathbed?" but the Foreign Secretary scuttled rabbit-like into the nearest shop, which unfortunately happened to sell *outré* lingerie.

When he came out, and as his oh-so-casual tour of the hideous, slum-like shopping precinct got under way, the attentive observer might have noted that, though the visiting party consisted of the Foreign Secretary, the Tory candidate, and a variety of Tory officials and policemen, the Foreign Secretary was never to be seen close to the Tory candidate, and the more Antony Craybourne-Fisk edged his way familiarly in the direction of the Foreign Secretary, the more that gentleman dived nervously at luckless shoppers, shook their hands and asked them what they'd been buying. (Most of the shoppers, having no notion who he was, conceived he must be something to do with market research, and one or two told him to mind his own business.) As they finished their twenty-minute stint, the Press asked for photographs, and the Foreign Secretary obliged, making no attempt to bring into the picture the candidate he was supposed to be in Bootham to support. Antony only got in, in fact, by dint of pushing his way forward to the Foreign Secretary's side and saying, "This will be one to show my grandchildren." Though how much the Foreign Secretary would mean to those putative grandchildren, when he meant so little to today's shoppers in Bootham, was anybody's guess.

All of which might have suggested, to the attentive observer, that the Foreign Secretary had been advised by someone at Conservative Central Office that there was, just possibly, something ever-so-*slightly* suspect about the Tory candidate for Bootham East, and that just in *case* anything came up in the future, it might be prudent to—well—to distance himself. Right?

The party around the Labour Leader had meanwhile taken themselves off to Somertown. Somertown had been canvassed and re-canvassed so often already by the Labour Party that it was feeling like a pile of old deckchairs, but in its grime and decrepitude it was felt to offer a poignant image of what Tory freedom led to, and one the Labour Leader had to be photographed against. The party split up, Jerry breezing off with the Leader, affable and chatty to emphasize his respectable, mainline Socialist credentials. Sue went off in the other direction with the Leader's wife. That lady was cheerful and friendly, but her clothes that February day were such dashing and splendid examples of sartorial radical chic that Sue felt drab by comparison. She was feeling pretty drab that day anyway, as it happened. Nor did she quite approve of the lady's campaign style: to stand on doorsteps and lecture semi-slum housewives on nuclear disarmament and the heroism of the Greenham Common women and their anti-Cruise campaign was to invite bewilderment and mutterings of "Well, I dunno, really . . . I mean, well . . . Well, yes, I'll think about it." But she was the Leader's wife, so Sue could do nothing about it but tag miserably along, feeling ever more inadequate with every doorstep. It didn't help, she thought, as she stood silent by, that so many windows in this hideous council dystopia were displaying Social Democrat or even Conservative election posters.

The Social Democrats themselves were having a splendid day. With a founding father and a founding mother of the movement in the town they were enjoying a wave of popular interest. Bread, circuses and not too much talk about politics was the Social Democrat formula. The leaders were wonderful in crowds, witty and friendly even when talking through a loud-hailer, and generally they made people feel good and well-disposed. Even Oliver Worthing felt good, and felt too that tiny spark of excitement and ambition without which nobody should enter politics. Oliver Worthing was wondering whether he might not, just possibly, make it.

For Oliver Worthing had been noticing and making calculations, and his calculations went like this: a left-wing Labour candidate always gets fewer votes than a moderate one. Where would the votes that he didn't get go? Not to the Tory candidate, assuredly. Again, that Tory candidate was clearly putting off wavering Tory voters rather than rallying them to his cause. He had obviously been the worst possible choice for a constituency like Bootham. In addition, the Bootham voters were apparently in a mood to tell the government that they expected them to do something more about unemployment than merely sitting on their well-padded backsides and saying: there is no alternative. Where were the votes of all these disaffected Tories to go? Not to a left-wing Labour candidate, assuredly.

I am in with a chance, Oliver Worthing said to himself. Do I want to be in with a chance? Do I want to go to Westminster—to all that hot air and whisky-breath, that flatulent oratory and bar-room barracking?

After his spot of canvassing the Labour Leader and the whole party went back to campaign headquarters. The Leader affected not to notice the slogan that had been spray-painted on the wall of the building, just by Jerry's warning to the media: PARANOIA RULES—OK? He met local party workers, and he met Jerry's team of keen young people from London. The two groups were as near literally as made no difference at daggers drawn, but for this encounter they smiled at the Leader and at each other, and they all said they were a great team, and in great heart. Then the Leader and the Leader's wife and Jerry and Sue and a party of other Labour functionaries went off to the Labour Club for a meal. The Leader was to speak at a rally that evening, but he was speaking first, as he had to go back to London to film a guest appearance on *Top of the Pops*.

Sue, from being vaguely unhappy about things, was beginning to feel disgruntled. As they all sat together at table, laughing and swapping stories, she felt dowdy and tongue-tied and inadequate, as she never felt on the doorsteps, talking to ordinary people. She had tried to ask Jerry what he wanted of her at the meeting tonight, but he'd just said, "Later, love," and gone into a deep huddle with the Leader. Sue felt nervous about tonight. It would be a big, public meeting, because of the Leader. There would be television, too, though admittedly they would have dismantled all their gear as soon as the Leader had finished. Anyway, it was an ordeal very different from a token five minutes at a Press conference. She didn't want to disturb Jerry, but . . . Oh, hell; he was the one who'd insisted that she come, wasn't he?

"Jerry."

"Not now, darling."

"Jerry. I want to know about tonight."

"Tonight?" (A male-complicity smile at the Leader as he disengaged himself, which the Leader was careful not to return, as his wife was watching.)

"Tonight. I'm supposed to be speaking."

"Speaking? Oh—so you are, darling. Well, I'm sure you'll do splendidly. You did last time."

"Last time was just Press. How long do you want me to speak for? When will I go on?"

"Oh, ten minutes, a quarter of an hour. Our good friend here will be on first, so we can't lay you on until—oh—nine, ten past or so."

"Just so long as I know. I think if you don't mind I won't come to the first part of the meeting. I'll just sit there getting more and more nervous."

"As you like, sweetie. Be there by quarter to nine, though."

And Jerry turned back to his high-political huddle with the Leader.

Sue boiled. That "sweetie" had been the last straw. She smiled a farewell to the Leader's wife, and at Jerry's hunched back, and excused herself from table. She walked out of the Labour Club, mouth set firmly, clutching the key of the hotel room. Really, Jerry was impossible. It wasn't as if she had wanted to come. He had insisted that she did. He had insisted that she had a contribution to make, from her own experience, and that she should speak about it. And now she was here, he had totally forgotten. Because the Leader was here—that Leader, by the by, whose compromises and shilly-shallying Jerry had condemned at every WRA Committee meeting, at every GLC council meeting, almost since the man was elected leader. Why tell her to come on the day the Leader was here, anyway? It occurred to her that it had been a rare example of Jerry's inefficiency. And it had happened because he didn't give a damn *when* she came, only *that* she came. She wasn't of use to him, politically; she was just there to be seen, as a wife. Just as any budding Tory candidate dragged his wife along to the selection committee, to have her looked over by the locals. An appendage. A decoration. Everything that Jerry had always affected to despise.

She sat for an hour in her hotel room, gloomily brooding. Then she slapped on some make-up and went out. She was going for a drink.

Superintendent Sutcliffe was sampling election meetings. He had been following up all day shadowy leads that had led nowhere, and he had toyed with the idea of driving back and dining at the Happy Dalesman. But their dinners had got progressively more disgusting as the election approached, for the landlord looked on the reporters as captive guests, quite unable to find anywhere else to stay as polling day loomed. The previous evening had been fish fingers and mashed potatoes, and the landlord's wife hadn't even had the grace to look apologetic. So Sutcliffe stayed in Bootham, had a pizza and a glass of wine, and went to the meetings on offer.

He took in the Conservative meeting first, because he felt that Antony Craybourne-Fisk was at the centre of his interest. The Foreign Secretary was speaking, and the audience was minuscule, for the Foreign Secretary had as much charisma as an earwig with a heavy cold, so Sutcliffe sat among about twenty pensioners who had come out to save on heating bills, and they all listened to a disquisition on Common Market regulations concerning animal fodder—not a subject well chosen for an industrial community. After ten minutes of watching Craybourne-Fisk sitting complacently at the Great Man's side, feigning intense absorption, Sutcliffe fled the meeting.

The Social Democrats in the Corn Exchange seemed

to be having a much jollier time. Lots of laughter and applause, and a general heady atmosphere of we-just-might-pull-it-off. On the platform with the celebrities Oliver Worthing seemed to cut a very slightly uneasy figure, as if he had a vague sense that politics ought to be a mite more serious than this. Or was it those rumours that, Sutcliffe had gathered from chatting to people around town, were beginning to be talked about more openly on the streets of Bootham? After twenty minutes of all this jolly-good-time, and before the speakers had actually got down to politics, Sutcliffe slipped out of the Corn Exchange.

He did feel like a drink, like a long pint of beer. Politics made him feel like that. He could understand why so many MPs spent long hours propping up the bar in the Palace of Westminster, getting three parts pissed before going off to deliver their totally automatic votes. So on his way to the Town Hall, where the Labour Party meeting was being held, he turned into the Lord Byron.

It wasn't a bad pub at all, and neither was the beer to be sneezed at. There was brass and red plush, and on the wall were pictures of prize fighters from the early nineteenth century, that still more brutal era of the first monetarists. The pub was no more than half full—little groups of laughing people—families, workmates. Which made the solitary woman over the gin and tonic stand out rather—or perhaps she would have anyway, for solitary elderly ladies are even today more common in pubs than solitary young women. And this one could not be more than—what?—thirty? Thirty-two? A good-looking woman, Sutcliffe decided, though not smart in any way; certainly not chic. But good features . . . familiar features. Sutcliffe remembered a picture, in the *Daily Mirror*, of a woman, smiling, but edgily, being met by a candidate . . . Of course!

As he watched he saw coursing down the woman's cheek a solitary tear. Equally suddenly, he saw her body racked by a violent single sob. They were isolated appearances; if he hadn't been watching he would not have noticed them. But this was, he decided, a very unhappy woman indeed. He took his drink over to her table.

"Would it help to talk about it?" he asked, adding as she looked up suspiciously: "I'm not a journalist. I won't pass anything you say on to the waiting millions. But I am a very good listener. It's part of my job."

"Are you a social worker?" Sue Snaithe asked.

"Sort of."

"Seems you can *be* one and *need* one, apparently," Sue said, with a trace of bitterness in her voice. "Do sit down. I'd like your company. But there isn't anything you can *do*."

"Well, anyway, I will sit down, even if only to be useless."

"You recognized me, I suppose. You mentioned journalists."

"That's right. I saw your picture in the *Mirror*."

"Oh, *that*! Loving wife comes to support battling husband. Jerry staged that, of course. He's very good at staging things—especially spontaneous happenings, spontaneous demonstrations, spontaneous expressions of outrage. Nobody would believe, from that picture, the sort of moral blackmail he went in for to get me to come up here."

"You don't want him to become an MP?"

"Oh—it's not that. Jerry would be an excellent MP—of a certain kind. He'd get things done. No—I didn't want to be involved with the *sort* of things that getting oneself elected involves: all the wheeling and dealing, and the arse-licking, and the conspiring. Above all, all the conspiring. It was by conspiring that Jerry got selected for this seat. I didn't have anything to do with that, of course, but it was pretty underhand stuff. I didn't want to have anything to do with the campaign either. I've got a job to do—a very demanding one, physically and emotionally—and Jerry does always go *on* about husbands and wives being separate and independent entities, and how disgraceful it is when wives are stuck up for people to look at, as if the whole thing were a beauty parade. All of which I agree with. But I should have noticed that when the WRA meets, it's always the women who make the coffee and sandwiches. If I had, it would have prepared me for what's happening now, which is a subtle adaptation of the traditional beauty parade of the wife. This one is designed to prove that our Jerry is a happy family man, and therefore couldn't—how could he?—be the left-wing bogeyman that the capitalist media depict him as. The fraudulence of it! And the moral blackmail he goes in for to get his way!"

"You know, I don't think you'd find your husband very different from other politicians in that respect."

"Then he should be! He talks as if he is!"

"You've twice used the expression 'moral blackmail.' What has he got to blackmail you with?"

"Oh—nothing really. It's a silly phrase, isn't it? Mostly when people use it, it just means putting emotional pressure on somebody. That's about what it is in this case. It really goes right back to when we met."

"How did you meet?"

"If you'll believe—in a cinema queue for *The Deer Hunters*. It blossomed quickly from there. Jerry seemed somehow all washed up then. He'd just left the army. He'd expected to make it his career, and suddenly, he said, it seemed a wrong direction to take. He didn't know the right direction, but he knew it wasn't in the army. I was just finishing my degree and going into social work, and as *we* got more and more involved, Jerry got more and more taken up with my work, and with my politics. So that as he's got further and further into Labour community politics, gone up and up in the GLC, he's always said: 'Thank God for you, Sue: you got me into this.' Or even, which is idiotic: 'I'm doing this for you.' "

"That doesn't make you happy?"

"I suppose it did, in a way, at first. Because Jerry became a different man. His life really seemed to have shape, a purpose. But now . . . I don't altogether like the idea that his politics are my politics. They may have been once, but they're not any longer. And the more he's got involved, the less the marriage has really meant to him. Now it's just something that fills the odd moments of his spare time. Oh—he comes home to me after the meetings. I suppose I should be grateful that he's not one of those fraternizers who go in for endless pub sessions, or casual affairs. He comes straight home. Rather a pathetic recommendation, really."

"You feel—what?—that you've been squeezed out?"

"Well, I feel more like the organ-grinder's monkey,

actually. You know, he goes on about wives being completely independent, having their own views and all that, but what if I went up there tonight and rubbished one of his and his kind's cherished views? What if I said I thought the nuclear disarmers were a lot of self-satisfied, misty-eyed loonies? Which I rather do, by the way. I think I'd find that I had independence—from *here* to *here*!"

With two fingers she delineated the limits of a very small space.

"Would you like another drink?" asked Sutcliffe.

"No. I've had two. That's my limit. If I go up there and wake Jerry up, I don't want him to be able to say that I was drunk."

"Is that what you're thinking of doing? Be careful: it could break up your marriage."

"I know. I know. Of course I will be careful. But sometimes I think I . . . that I don't even *like* Jerry any more. And that would be the end, wouldn't it? Oh Christ! Look over there!"

She was gazing at a slim, dark, intense young man who had just come in through the door.

"Who's that?"

"One of Jerry's London henchmen. One of the busiest toilers in the Socialist vineyard—a right little apprentice Machiavelli. Who do you think he's looking for? God! He's coming over."

"Sue?" the young man said heartily. "Jerry sent me over to fetch you. You're due on in twenty minutes."

"Oh? And how did Jerry know where to find me?"

"One of the lads saw you come in earlier."

"And reported it back to His Master," said Sue, her

voice loud and harsh. "CHRIST! It's like having a Mind-er. It's like living in a police state! I can understand what George Smiley's wife felt like! Get out of my bloody way!"

And, grabbing together her things, she marched fum-ing out of the pub.

"Women!" said the henchman of Jerry conspiratorially to Sutcliffe. He darted to the door of the pub and watched Sue's departing back as she walked down the street. "That's all right. She's gone into the Town Hall. I thought it would be better if I didn't accompany her."

"Tactful of you," said Sutcliffe.

"She seems to have got the feeling she's being watched."

"She does rather."

"Are you a sympathizer?" asked the infant Machia-velli.

"That's right," said Sutcliffe. (Two lies in one eve-ning, he thought. Still, he had voted Labour at every election until the last.) "I think I'll go along and listen to your lad. He sounds as if he's got what it takes."

"Oh, he has," said the beloved disciple, as they strolled in the direction of the Town Hall (smoke-blackened neo-Byzantine). "He's a politician to his fingertips. Of course, you might say he's outside his natural territory here. If this were London, everything would be sewn up, but it being the North—well, you can never tell with these people."

"In London he's got an organization behind him, has he?"

"All the way! It's the WRA who put him where he

is: they work with him, he works with them. When
the Leisure Activities Committee meets, the discussion
is just a formality, because what they're discussing on
Thursday has actually been decided at a WRA meeting
on Wednesday. He's brilliant, I tell you. And he's marvellous at involving the young, and the minorities, and
the women: he just drives them into activism."

"Really? From something his wife said, I rather
thought his attitude to women might be rather . . .
traditional."

"What an extraordinary thing to say! Sue must be
upset—nerves, I suppose. There's nobody done more
to give women preferential status in all the job openings
going. And he's poured money into lesbian groups."

"Ah," said Sutcliffe. "I must have misunderstood."

"He's one of the coming men. If he doesn't win this
seat, the party will just have to find him another. It'll
be criminal if he's lost to politics when they abolish the
Greater London Council."

"I rather thought he wouldn't need help from the
party—that he was pretty good at getting himself selected for seats."

The young man laughed.

"Oh yes, that's true enough. He organized the take-
over of the local party here. He knew the nomination
was his for the asking. He's a behind-the-scenes man
too, is our Jerry. No doubt what he did in Bootham,
he can do somewhere else!"

"Meanwhile," said Sutcliffe, as they turned into the
Town Hall, "He'll be doing his damnedest to get elected
here."

Jerry's endeavours to get elected, at that moment,

consisted of a stirring speech to a nearly full town
hall—an unusually large audience, assembled to hear
the Leader. The Leader had given a rather good
speech—impassioned, if lacking in specifics, and staying well this side of wind-baggery (as his predecessor
had invariably strayed to the other side of it). Jerry
was talking about democratization—democratizing the
levers of power, as he called it. Democracy, to Jerry,
meant democracy of the committed, all power to the
activists, and it thus had very little indeed to do with
real democracy, though since he didn't spell this out,
not everybody noticed. Another of his favourite words
was "elitism," which in his code language was used to
stigmatize anything from French food to pedigree dogs.
He managed to bring this in several times during his
speech as well. Sutcliffe, seeing him for the first time,
watched his performance with interest: a tall, healthy
man who radiated energy. However dubious the ideas,
he was putting them over with his whole body. So much
so, in fact, that there was just a suspicion of the ranter
in his speechifying—and there is nothing, in these times,
more calculated to put people off. There was another
odd thing about his speech, if you thought about it:
while in international affairs he seemed to be practically
a pacifist, in domestic ones he was exceedingly belli-
cose, and used words like "smash," "beat," "crush"
all the time. Sutcliffe wondered whether he was the
only one in the audience to notice the discrepancy.

As Snaithe reached the end of his speech, he turned
half in the direction of Sue, and his voice became lower,
even matey. It also lost its Standard Southern ring and
became coloured with a distinctly Yorkshire tinge. Why

not, after all? Had he not been brought up in York-shire?

"I'm going to ask my wife to have a few words with you. I haven't asked her up to see if you like the look of her. This election isn't about people's looks, or their wives' looks, it's about policies. And I haven't asked her up here to say what a fine bloke I am, either. Nor is she up here to repeat my views. She has her ideas, I have mine, and Sue's no glove puppet, I can assure you of that. She's come up here today because she thinks that her experience—among the poorest and most under-privileged in one of the poorest London boroughs—is pretty relevant to what you can all see around you in Bootham today. And I think it tells you something pretty important about how Tory freedom works . . . and in whose benefit it works."

Sue got a sympathetic round of applause. She began speaking of some of her experiences in Hackney, in a low voice, getting attention by the starkness of the distress she had witnessed. Jerry sat back in his hard little seat, his face a mask of intense interest that didn't quite conceal his satisfaction. He'd rather forgotten her, in the excitement of the Leader's visit, but he'd done well to get her up here. She was really being very useful.

But after a few minutes, Sue strayed on to wider issues.

"I don't want to talk about these people as cases. They're not cases, they're not problems, they're peo-ple. And I sometimes think it would be a better country to live in if we listened now and then to what they said, what they were thinking. Jerry here's been talking about democracy. Fine. But none of the parties believes in putting the issues directly to the people—by referenda, for example. And yet, in this electronic day and age it would be a perfectly simple thing to do. Why shouldn't ordinary people have their say about local government reorganization, about schools—yes, about hanging, about nuclear disarmament too?"

Jerry's mask of a face had become a good deal more tense. The brothers certainly did not believe in referenda. That wasn't their idea of democracy, Good heavens no! My God!—*think* what people would probably vote for! You'd never get any truly radical ideas through their thick skulls! Sutcliffe saw Jerry's hand on his right leg begin a rhythmic, involuntary tapping on his knee. She had strayed outside that space from *here* to *here* that constituted her freedom of opinion.

"Yes—why shouldn't ordinary people have their say, directly, about nuclear disarmament, the most important subject of all? My opinion on that, by the way, is a bit different from Jerry's." (The drumming of the fingers became heavier, more insistent. Nuclear disarmament was a matter of holy writ.) "Personally I think the only thing that matters is general disarmament. I think it's daft for Britain to think disarming unilaterally would make a scrap of difference—as daft as those people in Sheffield who've declared the town a nuclear free zone." ("Christ," said Jerry's henchman, beside Sutcliffe. "The cow!") "It's just silliness to think you can contract out like that. And I strongly suspect that most ordinary people would agree with me. But the point I want to make is that it's possible to *ask* ordinary people what they think about things like that. And the more you ask them, the more they will stop thinking of themselves as helpless, as the cast-offs of society, just voting-fodder at election-time, despised in non-election years. They might even feel themselves to be real parts of a living democracy . . ."

And Sue went on in this vein for some time. And as Sutcliffe slipped out of the hall, his last view of the party on the dais was of those taut, tense, muscular fingers of Jerry's, tap-tap-tapping on his knees as he hid his irritation at Sue's perfidy beneath a mask of polite interest in her opinions.

13

The Alliance
Candidate

The night air was good, after so much
hot air. Whatever the streets of Bootham were normally
like at nine-thirty on a weekday evening—and Sutcliffe
imagined they must be pretty dead apart from the strains
of music from some degraded disco or other—tonight
there was a fair concourse of people, and a faint hum
of talk. Some had come out behind him from the Town
Hall, and had dashed for the nearest phone: getting the
story of Sue's declaration of dissent to London for the
late editions, Sutcliffe guessed, for the Labour meeting
had held a fairly high proportion of media people to a
fairly low proportion of real ones. There were other
people around too, though, quite a few streaming from
the direction of the Corn Exchange: jolly, middle-class
people, mostly coming from the Social Democratic
jamboree. Did that augur badly for the Conservative vote in Antony Craybourne-Fisk's natural class-
catchment area?

Curiosity impelled Sutcliffe to stroll towards the Corn
Exchange, and he was just in time to see the two guest

speakers saying their farewells to a little knot of supporters, and tearing themselves away and into their taxis
as if it was the dearest wish of both of them to return
to Bootham at the earliest possible opportunity. Sutcliffe strolled on, but on an impulse he looked back,
and saw that the little knot of Social Democrats had
evaporated, leaving the tall, lean, rather lost figure of
Oliver Worthing looking around him uncertainly on
the grey pavement. Sutcliffe turned back.

"Mr Worthing?"

"Yes?"

"My name is Sutcliffe. You won't know me, but you
may have heard of me: I'm in Bootham looking into
the death of James Partridge."

"Oh—ah—yes." Oliver Worthing looked at him with
frank interest. "Actually, I had heard. No doubt we
all have. You can't expect something like that not to
get talked about, especially during a by-election."

"I was wondering—I know this is a lot to ask—if
we could have a talk somewhere, some time. I'm willing
to fit it in any time that suits your schedule."

"I'm afraid that means breakfast-time or late at night.
But what about now? I'm just wondering where I left
my car. We could go back to my flat and have some
coffee."

"That would be splendid, if you're not too exhausted."

"I'm like a worn-out dishcloth, but I'll be this way
until polling day. I wonder, did I leave my car down
by the swimming pool?"

In the event, he had. On the way to his flat in a
middle-class suburb of Bootham they talked about the
meeting, the prospects for the Social Democrats, the

feeling on the doorsteps. They didn't get on to the topic
in hand until they were in Oliver Worthing's kitchen
and he was making coffee.

"Instant, I'm afraid. The penalty of accepting coffee
with a 'new bachelor.' "

"Is that the expression? I take it you're divorced."

"That's right. I'm a single-parent family who's lost
his family—the most deprived and unsympathized-with
group there is. Perhaps if I get in I'll put together a
private member's bill to give them some rights. Yes,
my wife left me not long after the last election. Things
had been falling apart before then, but the political
involvement didn't help. It tends to be a full-time thing,
or nothing. We're still friends. That's what they all say
these days, isn't it? What does it amount to? She sends
me a card on my birthday, and I send her one a day
or two after hers. We're polite when I go round for
the kids. I gather the Partridges broke up too."

"That's right."

"They kept it pretty quiet. I never heard rumours—
and these things get about, as a rule, even across party
lines. Was it just a trial separation?"

"In name. She was doing a minimum of wifely things
until Christmas, in case he had second thoughts. But
I haven't come across anything to suggest that he was
having them. Did you know him well? Did you know
him at all?"

"Good question. Usually you don't do much more
than glimpse your opponents at the final count. Here
you are with your names coupled day after day on TV
or radio, and you never meet. I did have a *little* more
to do with Partridge than that."

"Why was that?"

"There were one or two small things connected with the Council—I'm on the Health Committee, and he was at the Ministry for a time. Mostly small things that were settled by phone. The only time I actually went to see him was about a student at College—a very bright girl, desperate to go to university. Her father— filthy rich garage owner—refused to chip in his contribution: didn't believe in girls going to university, wasted when they got married, you know the kind of garbage. Jim Partridge got it settled very quietly and tactfully. He could have made more fuss about it, elevated it to a matter of principle, but then the girl would probably never have gone to Cambridge."

"What about the General Election campaign? Was it a friendly fight? A good, clean campaign?"

"Ah," said Oliver Worthing, handing Sutcliffe a cup and leading the way into the living-room. "So you've heard the rumours?"

"I've heard whispers of rumours."

"Erroneous whispers, no doubt." The two sat down, and Worthing gulped thirstily at his coffee. "The answer to your question is: yes, it was a good, clean campaign. And it was so thanks mainly to Jim Partridge."

"Ah—so you've reason to be grateful to him."

"I have. Though since the rumours are idiotic distortions of the truth I sometimes think I might as well issue a public statement giving the facts. I would have done so this time, but my agent said it would be political suicide."

"What actually happened last time?"

"Oh, somebody brought the rumours over from Rotherham, where I was born and brought up. Naturally he shared his information with one or two others among the Tory bigwigs, and they buzzed around with it to a few more, and wanted to make it a campaign issue. There are one or two very unpleasant sods among the high-ups in the local party. Walter Abbot, for example—ah, you know him. Well, of course they took the rumour to Harold Fawcett, and I think he would have gone along with it—he's an average, quarter-way decent individual, is Harold, and no great shakes morally. But of course he took it to Jim Partridge first, and Jim killed it stone dead, squashed it flat—but *flat*. Said he was not going to get elected with help of a dirty tricks department, that he'd publicly dissociate himself from any attempt to use the rumour, and so on. He was a gentleman, I realize that: an old-fashioned kind of gentleman. Perhaps that's why he never really seemed at home in the modern Conservative Party."

"I think you're right. But these rumours have surfaced again. Does that mean that Mr Craybourne-Fisk is all too at home in the modern Conservative Party?"

"No, I don't think so. I suspect that Harold Fawcett, for mere shame, felt he couldn't use them this time, after Jim's veto. All our information suggests they're being spread this time by the Labour people. Mind you, I don't think they've got very far with them, and from now on they'll be very much on the defensive about that kind of thing."

"Oh? Why's that?"

"Haven't you seen the evening papers? No, I suppose you wouldn't see the *Bootham Evening Post*." He grabbed a copy of the paper from a side table. "They've got an interview with that thug the Labour Party employed to terrorize the media. Obliging chap now, apparently: always ready to talk to the media. His 'I'm White' tattoo, he told the *Post*, is some sort of code slogan for a little Fascist offshoot grouping, dedicated to duffing up any member of the immigrant community it doesn't like the look of. He says his aim is to "Keep the blackies out of the pits"—odd that, I felt, in view of the nature of the work. Anyway, he's got a record: two cases of aggravated assault, a string of minor offences, all against coloureds. Says he's been a keen supporter of the Labour Party all his life. Pathetic, isn't it? Without wishing to be calculating, that interview will be worth five hundred to a thousand votes to us. *And* Mr Jerry Snaithe won't be spreading rumours about Borstal and criminal records in the near future."

"Have you any evidence it has been Snaithe?"

Oliver Worthing shrugged.

"Him or his henchmen. There's a thin dividing line between what he tells them to do, and what they do knowing he'd be in favour. The London far left mob has a very bad reputation for spreading unsubstantiated or misleading rumours."

"And is this one without foundation?"

"It's *untrue*. But it's not without foundation." He leaned forward in his chair, his face troubled. "Here's the whole story. I don't like talking about it, but I realize you've got ways of finding out—and once in a while, talking about it is therapeutic. What connection it could have with James Partridge's death is beyond me. I was brought up in Rotherham, as I told you, and my father was a schools inspector there—a pleasant, inoffensive man with a conscience. My mother made his life hell. She was a woman—I try to look back on her objectively now, though it's difficult—with a vile, simmering temper. The whole house was tense with it, twenty-four hours a day, waiting to see whether it would break out, or confine itself to jibes and pin-pricks and expressions of grievance. You can imagine the atmosphere in the house. My father, my sister, myself—all waiting, watching for some explosion, for one of those red-hot blazes of temper. She nursed grudges for months, and then suddenly out they would come in some searing stream of hatred. I don't know how my father could stand it. And the long and the short of it is—I couldn't."

"What happened?"

"I exploded. In the only way I could. I couldn't fight her verbally—it had to be physical."

"How old were you?"

"Just turned fourteen. One of the blazing tempers was just reaching a climax, and I simply threw myself on her with whatever weapon happened to be to hand. It was a poker, actually—but a heavy, iron one, and I just kept hitting her. The front door was open—it was summer—and she ran screaming into the street, face running blood, and the neighbours naturally rang the police. There wasn't much chance of keeping it within the family after that; probably wouldn't have been anyway, because she was seriously hurt. The police weren't bad about it. I don't think they really knew what to do. They took me into custody, questioned me, then lodged me in a children's home while they waited for medical reports and went into the family background. The children's home is the origin of the 'Borstal' sneer, of course. It was a pretty tough place, actually, but a haven of peace after my home. Eventually my father's sister said she'd take me in. She was a big, cheerful woman with several kids of her own. My father paid her, of course, and I think she was glad of the money, but I was always grateful to her. I lived there until I went to university, and I always regarded it as my home."

"Did you ever see your mother again?"

"Once. When my father was dying. She didn't speak to me. She was a woman utterly without self-knowledge. I believe she urged the police to press charges. Later on she devoted herself to ruining my sister's life. I feel guilty about that: I snapped and got away, and my life turned out—well—middling to all right. She stood it, year after year, and her life was ruined. She never married, because Mother scared anyone off. She worked at a dreary job, and she's still at it, twisted and sick. Yes, I feel guilty about that . . . As a matter of fact, people who know me well say that I can feel guilty about almost anything under the sun."

"Because of the attack on your mother?"

"I'm not an amateur psychiatrist, but it's a fair bet, isn't it? I worry particularly about my own children, of course. Though, God knows, their home life was never anything like mine, even while the marriage was crumbling apart. And these days being the children of divorced parents is hardly rare, or any sort of stigma. But—I worry about them constantly, would ring my ex-wife up every other night if I thought she'd stand for it . . . Well, that's me. That's what people are whispering about."

"You don't think of putting out a statement?"

"Yes, I've thought about it, as I said. But my agent says it would do much more harm than good at this stage of the campaign. Inevitably it would be played up by the gutter press. And in fact I've got a good local reputation, through my years on the council, and the job at the College. Quite a lot of my voters have been through my hands there, or have children who have, and I think their word will stand up against all the rumour-mongers."

"The fact remains that you have reason to be grateful to James Partridge."

"I do. That's why I don't quite understand your interest. I suppose in a case like this you have to check all possibilities."

"Exactly. That's what all cases involve: slog over irrelevancies. One little irrelevancy: what were you doing the evening he died?"

"That's easy. I was at a college council meeting. I remember because I reported there on the case of the girl who had a scholarship to Cambridge—the thing Jim Partridge sorted out for us. I felt quite sick next morning when I heard he was dead."

"Everything I hear suggests he was an admirable chap."

"As far as I'm concerned, I would say he had an instinctive moral sense that told him what should and shouldn't be done. It's pretty rare in a politician—practically unknown these days."

"As witness Jerry Snaithe."

"Or his henchmen. I gain pleasure from the fact that they do a great deal more harm to themselves than good. I loathe the idea of a candidate coming in with a little posse of disciples. I gather you can cut the atmosphere at the Labour Party HQ with a knife—the old North-South divide in miniature. I must say I have one great advantage in this campaign which I didn't have last time: I have two very dislikeable opponents."

"You don't know the Conservative?"

"No, indeed. But he is getting known locally as a prize shit. He is one of the yes-men at Conservative Central Office, hoping to be one of the yes-men in Parliament, then one of the yes-men in government. People always talk about the Prime Minister as tough, but I don't think it's tough to surround yourself with pipsqueaks, do you? Have you talked to Craybourne-Fisk yet, Superintendent?"

"Not yet. I have that pleasure to come."

"Because there are one or two rumours going around about *him*."

14

Tory Hopeful

Breakfast-time, Sutcliffe had learnt from Oliver Worthing, was one of the only times when one could hope to find a candidate alone, so it was at breakfast-time next day that he went back to Moreton-in-Kirkdale, to try and have a few words with Antony Craybourne-Fisk.

Antony's breakfast had been made for him by Mrs Burkshaw from the next cottage. Antony was one of the last males in his generation to have been brought up totally unable to fend for himself, and to have remained in this benighted state thus far into his adulthood. If he had been forced to make his own breakfast he might have managed to pour milk on cereal, to butter bread and spread marmalade on it, but further than that—even to a boiled egg, or toast—he could not have gone. Fortunately Mrs Burkshaw's late husband had been a farm labourer and she was used to getting up at the crack of dawn, so that when he asked her if she could cook something nourishing for him early she had been glad to. She had quoted a sum in recompense so low that Antony had jumped at it without haggling. Perhaps, he had thought, there might be compensations in living part of the year in England's cheapest county.

"I'll be glad of the money," Mrs Burkshaw said later, in the village shop, "but I can't say I took to him. Any more than I took to that Mrs Partridge—even at the beginning, when she was trying to be nice."

People in general, it seemed, were not taking to Antony. As he ate his breakfast that morning the crease-lines on his forehead showed that he was worried. He himself had detected, from the beginning of the campaign, a lack of warmth towards him even from long-standing Conservative voters. He and Harold Fawcett had kept quiet about it for a time, but there was no disguising it now, with the campaign entering its last week. The latest humiliation had been to overhear a discussion in the loo at Tory Party Headquarters as to whether he would or would not be pushed into third place. Third place! It was unthinkable! And yet it had happened to the Conservative candidate at Chesterfield, who was a much more endearing young man than he was. (This was not quite how Antony Cray-bourne-Fisk put it to himself, but he was not unaware that among his political assets charm was his short suit.)

And there was another thing that was bothering Antony. He had been aware from the beginning of the campaign that the distinguished politicians who came to Bootham ostensibly to give him a hand were in fact keeping him at arm's length. Conservative Headquarters, while ostensibly pouring in support, was in innumerable little ways distancing itself from him as candidate. It was damned unfair! He had, against his better judgment, allowed them to send up seven or eight members of the dreariest cabinet in human memory, and then they treated him as if he had a mild attack of leprosy. Why? Why?

In his lonely meditations on his satin-eiderdowned bed in the Partridge cottage Antony Craybourne-Fisk had been forced to the conclusion that there had been Rumours. Leaks and rumours had bedevilled this government. Only the previous year rumour had nearly destroyed one of its most senior members—apparently quite untrue rumours. If they didn't even have to be true . . . ! As to leaks, the government had lived by leaks and eventually could well die by them. Once one had faced up to the fact that one was being talked about in muffled tones, it needed no ingenuity to connect the rumours with the presence in Bootham of a Scotland Yard detective. Would the man want to interview him? It was a situation that would require the utmost care in its handling. Antony decided that if the policeman should come to see him, he would be nice. Tremendously nice. Unnaturally nice. It would be worth the effort.

Thus it was that when Sutcliffe knocked on the door of the cottage on the Thursday before polling day, Antony (who had watched him arrive, and guessed who it was) was smiling bonhomously in welcome even when he went to open the door. The smile disconcerted Sutcliffe: it was a bit like meeting Oliver Hardy when you were expecting Stan Laurel.

"Good morning, sir. I hope I'm not disturbing you. I'm Superintendent Sutcliffe. I wonder if I could have a few words with you?"

"Of course, Superintendent. I was wondering if you would need to. Come right in. Cup of tea? There's one left in the pot, and it should be reasonably warm."

It wasn't reasonably warm, but Sutcliffe took it, and settled himself down in one of those over-large arm-chairs, preparing to play the interview the way Antony seemed to want it.

"I haven't asked what your business is, you notice," the Tory candidate said, spearing efficiently into his mouth the last fragments of his fried breakfast. "There have been rumours of a policeman going round asking questions about Jim Partridge."

"That's right. That's what I've been doing."

"Meaning, presumably, that the police are still not satisfied?"

"Something of the sort," Sutcliffe said. He decided to be very vague. This was no time, for example, to admit that he was in fact on holiday. "We're in a difficult position: we have no pin-downable grounds for dissatisfaction, yet on the other hand we have no particular reason to be satisfied. We have found no motive for suicide, for example—not one that we think holds water."

"You don't think the breakdown of his marriage—?"

"It had happened some time before. It seems to have been coming on for some time, and he appears to have taken it very calmly. That's our information. Perhaps you yourself know more about it, sir?"

"Me?" Antony's Adam's apple bobbed up and down like a skiff in choppy seas.

"As a close friend of Mrs Partridge's."

"Ah—I see—well, I don't know that I—"

"Hadn't you better tell me, sir, something about that friendship with Mrs Partridge?"

Oh, that friendship with Mrs Partridge! How bitterly to be regretted now, the more so as it had never meant particularly much to him at any moment of its duration. How to explain to a policeman that one slipped into these things, especially on aimless vacations, and in run-down, once-fashionable hotels in Italy? They had both been staying, separately, at the Hotel Splendido in Santa Margherita Ligure. It was the end of the season, and the only other guests had been Italian or German, and they had sat dotted around ten or twelve tables in the enormous dining-room, and the atmosphere had been soporific. It was September, and the break-up of Penelope Partridge's marriage had just become an established fact. In the mornings she took the children to sit by but not to bathe in that putrid section of the Mediterranean. Sometimes in the afternoons she would take them to Portofino, or went up to Genoa to shop. It was in Portofino, at an outdoor café, that Antony had first talked to her, though he had noticed her across those expanses of dining-room, and had registered that she was of his kind, had "sniffed the exhalation of his own herd." They had come together out of boredom, slept together for the same reason, and because "why not?" They had discovered common interests—money and power—and had established and rejoiced in a common coldness of heart. When Antony had promised to take charge of the financial side of the separation, and to help her with quick kill investments after the settlement was made, an alliance was made between them that had never been broken. Unfortunately.

This, or a judicious selection from this, was what
Antony told Sutcliffe.

"I see," said the Superintendent, when the bland and
blameless recital had come to an end. "And you still
manage her investments?"

"That's right."

"Is this an arduous task? Much to invest?"

"There's a tidy little nest-egg that she inherited from
her mother, and there's money that Partridge settled
on her when they split up. Together it comes to a
substantial sum."

"Does that mean she milked him for all she could
get?"

"That's a rather tendentious phrase, isn't it, Superintendent? It was a perfectly amicable separation. She
had worked hard to make his career a success. And
Partridge would naturally wish to ensure that the children were well provided for."

"And how have you invested this? Gilt-edged?"

"Not entirely, Superintendent. Mrs Partridge enjoys
a bit of excitement, relishes the element of risk. We've
been living a bit dangerously with some of the
money—hoping to increase it substantially."

"And have you?"

"Yes," said Antony, with an immodest smirk.

"You've been living dangerously in other ways too,
haven't you?"

"I beg your pardon?"

"You left something out of your account of your
friendship with Mrs Partridge, didn't you. The weekends at country hotels . . ."

Antony looked as if he would dearly have liked to

give way to a spurt of venom, but he was a well-trained
political animal, and he merely smiled a somewhat
strained smile, and stretched out his legs underneath
the table.

"Ahhh . . . Who could have told you about that, I
wonder. That mountain of Scandinavian muscle that
looks after the kids, I suppose. Well, I can't say I wanted
it to come out, but equally I can't say I'm particularly
ashamed of it. We're both men of the world, I take it,
Superintendent?"

"Yes, sir. But you're a rather younger man of the
world than I am."

"Meaning that fashions in what is on the edge of
permissibility change, I suppose? I take your point. As
far as my generation is concerned, I don't think anyone
would see anything at all remarkable in my spending
the weekend now and again with a rather lonely
woman—on a no-strings basis."

"Is that all it is, sir? A casual affair of convenience?"

"Oh, absolutely. Absolutely. There's never been any
question of its developing into anything serious. Of
course, as things have turned out . . . with my getting
the nomination here . . ."

"Yes?"

"Well, one rather regrets . . . I mean, retrospectively
it doesn't seem to have been awfully wise. But of course
at the time Jim Partridge was alive, and so there didn't
seem . . ."

"Quite. If you were that careful, all Tory MPs' wives
would be taboo, wouldn't they, sir? Well, I imagine
you'll soon be wanting to get along?"

Antony looked at his watch.

"Well, yes, I would, rather . . ."

"Just one more question before you get back to the hustings: do you happen to remember what you were doing on the night Mr Partridge died—December the twelfth it was."

"Good Lord, no—so long ago. Wait, though. I may still have last year's diary." He dived across the room, and rummaged in a briefcase. "Yes. Here it is. The twelfth, you say? Here we are. Oh yes: I was addressing a local Tory association—in Deptford. Meeting began at seven-thirty."

"And when did it end, sir?"

"Haven't a clue. I do a lot of that sort of meeting: the Conservative Central Office sends me round as a peripatetic speaker. On form, it would have ended round about nine-thirty or ten. When was Jim . . . When did Jim die?"

"That we're not sure about. There's something to connect it to a time around ten-thirty or so, but it's very slight. All we know is that when it was found the body had been in the water for hours."

"I see . . . Not very satisfactory . . . Well, Superintendent—"

"Quite. I realize you're busy, sir. I think we've gone as far as we can at the moment . . ."

Some faint spurt of cynicism impelled Sutcliffe thus to imply that he had not finished with Antony. That might take the shine out of his campaigning! But whether that gentleman noticed, Sutcliffe was not quite sure, for he had bustled himself out, locked the door behind them both, and got himself into his car after the briefest of waves. He was off down the lane before Sutcliffe had even extracted his car keys from his mac pocket.

"Excuse me."

Oh Lord: it was the inquisitive neighbour, who might well feel a grievance against him for his deception of her last time. Still, better not pass up the opportunity for a chat. He had had the feeling that she was a sharp-witted, observant person.

"You're the man who pretended to be Mrs Partridge's friend."

"Not quite. If you go over what I actually said—"

"Don't worry. I have. And it was a bit borderline, to put it politely. I still think you got into that cottage under false pretences."

"It was a question of time. I'm a policeman. I only had to go away and get a warrant, or permission from Mrs Partridge. I'm afraid I took a short cut."

"Oh, I see,' said Mrs Burkshaw, mollified. "So you're police, are you? I *did* wonder . . . Investigating his death, I suppose?"

"That's right."

"And talking to Mr Fisk. I shouldn't have thought there could be any connection there . . . could there?"

She was fishing. Sutcliffe kept a smiling silence, then asked:

"What's your opinion of him?"

"I do breakfasts for him. I'm glad to have the work."

Sutcliffe was not the only one who could keep mum.

"Will you be voting for him?"

"Not on your life! I've never voted Tory in all my days, except the once, and that was personal—for Mr Partridge. Here—you know I told you about them men coming round at night?"

"Yes. Have they been again?"

"Yes. No. Well—not like *that*. It's just that two

nights ago . . . much earlier this time, around ten
o'clock—I looked out of my window, and in the lane
I saw this van. Well, I'm not an expert, but it looked
just the same shape as the van that had been there that
night. There were lights on in the cottage. Now, I
didn't want to do any nosey-parkering—"

"No, no."

"—but I thought they might be breaking in. So I
went out, very nervous, like—it's *that* dark at nights
around here—and I saw at once that they weren't likely
to be breaking in, because Mr Fisk's car was parked
further along. But I just walked towards the cottage a
bit, to make certain all was all right, and sure enough
it was: Mr Fisk was talking in his living-room with
another man—a big chap."

"Ah yes."

"But I thought you might like to know what it said
on the side of the van. It said: MANOR COURT FARM
LTD."

"Yes," said Sutcliffe. "I rather thought it might."

15

Tory Helpfuls

Night after night, as the date of the Bootham by-election approached, the television news programmes had by-election specials, with their reporters filing breathless copy against a background of gas works, slum council flats, or one of the innumerable disused factories. "More relevant," the reporters told their cameramen. It was estimated that one in ten of the inhabitants of Bootham had been interviewed, some of them more than once, and some of them so often that they had in the end threatened physical violence towards the interviewer.

All this was, when one came to think about it, a quite factitious excitement, for the government had a majority so large that no mere by-election loss in an area that was remote from Tory heartland was likely (in a sane world) to cause more than a shrug of the shoulders. But politics is not a sane world, and politicians as well as political commentators were indeed looking to Bootham, as complacent publicans in the constituency so often pronounced them to be.

And yet, the more excitement hotted up in Bootham, the more it began to live up to its description as a political cynosure, the more Sutcliffe wondered whether his work there might not for the moment be finished. Some sort of pattern, or patterns, was beginning to form in his mind, but to get them fully into focus he felt he had to turn elsewhere. For James Partridge had been no more than an occasional visitor to Bootham, and the centre of his life had been in London. One night in his miserable little room in the Happy Dalesman, Sutcliffe took out his notebook; he tabulated some of his facts and ideas, and then he wrote down a list of the people he would like to see or speak to. The next day he happily handed in his key, and set his car towards the Smoke.

The first day back in London he spent in moderately fascinating routine. He was on vacation, on final, pre-retirement leave, and his activities were his own choice. He drove to the South Bank and to the library of County Hall, where he spent an interesting half-hour leafing through the minutes of the Leisure Activities Committee—interesting because of what was *not* said, rather than what was: every meeting seemed to demand no more than a bald statement of decisions taken, followed by "The meeting closed at 9:40," or "The meeting was adjourned at 9:30." They were never much longer than two hours, these meetings, and why should they be? Had not all the decisions been taken in advance? How easy to proclaim the virtues of open government when that was the case!

Sutcliffe spoke over the phone to a policeman in Rotherham who remembered the Oliver Worthing case, back in the early 'fifties. It had made a real impression on him. "At first glance it seemed like a particularly vicious business, and the boy nothing short of a thug," he recalled; "but you only had to have a few words with the mother and you began to have sympathy with the lad." Sutcliffe looked into Jeremy Grayling-Snaithe's military career, found out that he had been in the SAS, and had a long and meaty chat with his commanding officer, since retired: "Of course we need people who can go in with all guns blazing if necessary, but we can do without people who want to do it all the time. It's a question of instinct, and he didn't have it. It was his judgment that was in question," the Colonel added, in an unconscious echo of the Amplehurst monk.

Sutcliffe's cunningest move was to ring the Chairman of the Conservative Party. After several layers of Roedean, he got through.

"Ah—Good morning, sir. I'm glad to find you in. I thought perhaps you might be up in Bootham."

"No. Actually I *thought* I might have to be up there quite a bit during the campaign, but as it's turned out . . ."

"You've preferred not to? Found it better to distance yourself from the candidate?"

The chairman, ignoring the slight note of impertinence, let out a little squeal of dissent.

"Oh *no*, Inspector—Superintendent—no, I *assure* you—that's quite a wrong impression you've got there."

"Is it, sir? I've been lodging with a pack of journalists, all very experienced in these campaigns, and I'm afraid that's the impression they've got. That the party top brass has preferred to keep its distance."

"But that's nonsense! We've absolutely *poured* top people into the constituency!"

"But that was all arranged before we had our previous talk, wasn't it, sir? Once they get there, they seem to have preferred to keep their distance from the candidate. I take it that, if you had the selection process to do all over again, you wouldn't be pushing Mr Craybourne-Fisk *quite* so hard, am I right?"

"That could be, Superintendent. But that's because you—"

"Because I found out his connection with Mrs Partridge. Quite. In fact, I suspect there is quite a lot to be found out about Mr Craybourne-Fisk that might be electorally disadvantageous. To you, I mean. Tell me, sir: why was he pushed by Conservative Central Office?"

"Well, the PM . . . Actually, the word came from higher up."

"I see. Is Mr Craybourne-Fisk personally known Higher Up, or do you think there was some lobbying on his behalf by someone who has the ear of On High?"

"Well . . . personally I blame Derek Manders."

"Ah—he would be a friend of the candidate, I take it."

"Very close. Thick as—very close. And Manders is Well Liked—higher up."

"And involved with Mr Craybourne-Fisk financially too, I take it?"

The Chairman, who had become confiding on wings of grievance, suddenly clammed up.

"That I wouldn't know about."

"Thank you, sir. You've told me all I wanted to know."

Derek Manders, MP, when Sutcliffe spoke to him on the phone, sounded a lordly young man, whose lordliness slid into a sort of affability when he heard what Sutcliffe's mission was. The policeman was invited for coffee at the gentleman's Mayfair residence the next morning. There he sat in luxurious plush, from the depths of which he could watch Derek Manders himself—all long legs and good tailoring and gleaming brown leather shoes.

"Antony?" The voice was Oxford and the City, and grated on Sutcliffe, perhaps because the arrogance seemed to have so flimsy a basis. "Oh no, not a *close* friend. By no means. In fact, you know, I rather doubt whether he *has* any close friends. But we've had contacts, you know, over financial matters, as one does."

Sutcliffe suppressed the inclination to say "Does one?" and merely murmured: "Quite."

"He's something of a whiz-kid in City matters, you know. The golden touch, in a modest kind of way." He looked around his sitting-room, as if to say there were golden touches and golden touches. "As a matter of fact that happens to be my form of bingo too. So we've been . . . thrown together, on occasion."

"I see, sir. I gather Mr Craybourne-Fisk has been handling such matters for James Partridge's wife as well."

"So I hear. Of course that's perfectly normal—one of his sidelines, in fact. But still . . . I knew nothing about that, I may say; otherwise I'd have hesitated to . . . well . . ."

"To recommend him as candidate for the Bootham seat?"

"Ah, you know about that. Well, yes. And there's the personal involvement, which is even worse. I've taken a fair bit of stick over that, I can tell you."

"From Higher Up?"

"Precisely. But all I knew about were Antony's own

financial dealings, which were always above board. Very sharp, sometimes a bit close to the wind, but above board. Almost always."

Mr Manders was clearly distancing himself from Antony by being prepared to come remarkably clean, doubtless about everything except his own involvements with him. Sutcliffe prepared to take advantage of the frankness.

"Only almost always, sir?"

"Well, there was a business about shares in British Telecom—there were whispers about that. I suspect that he got *far* more shares than he was legally entitled to, and went for a quick killing. He knows all the dodges, and then some. He started very modestly, you know: rather ambiguous family background, and no *money* that you could call money. But he must be worth a tidy sum now."

"There's a factory farmer in the constituency called Abbot. You wouldn't know of any connection—financial connection, for example—between the two, would you?"

"Good Lord, no. I don't know any *detail* about Antony's affairs. But of course a lot of shares with animal connections did dip a bit when the details of the Animals' Charter were published. Not significantly, you realize, since there were doubts about the bill ever becoming law, but still, certainly a drop. Cosmetics, factory farming, the fur trade. Antony could have bought, being pretty certain that if the bill became law, all the teeth would have been removed, as far as commercial concerns went. We would have seen to that."

"We?"

"The Tory MPs with City connections . . . with the commercial health of the country at heart."

Derek Manders, as he made his emendation, gave Sutcliffe a swift glance of complicity, as if they were in a game together. After all, policemen were always Tory, weren't they?

"I ask about factory farmers," resumed Sutcliffe, "because Mr Craybourne-Fisk seems to be in contact with this pretty large factory farmer in his constituency."

"Does he? Not necessarily anything significant in that. Antony would naturally get in touch with all the business leaders in the area. Any Tory candidate would."

"But this was a man who was on very bad terms with James Partridge, over the animals bill."

Derek Manders shrugged.

"So what? Nothing very surprising there. Antony and Jim Partridge were a very different kind of Tory. Jim was the 'sixties version, Antony the later 'seventies or 'eighties version. Very little in common. They wouldn't have found a lot to talk about if they were thrown together."

"Beyond, perhaps, Mrs Partridge."

Derek Manders gave an appreciative, lop-sided smile.

"Beyond the lovely Penelope. Who, while her husband sailed the perilous seas at Westminster and Bootham, did *not* stay at home and peg away at her tapestry. Not one for home industries, our Penelope."

"Tell me," said Sutcliffe, getting up, "did *you* know James Partridge well?"

"No. Not well at all, I'm afraid."

"Was he a man of few close friends as well?"

"Oh no, I don't think so. Well—*few*, perhaps, but he did *have* close friends, unlike Antony. There was Terry Stopford, for example: one was always seeing Jim and Terry together in the Commons restaurant, or the bar."

"I've heard the name. He's an MP, isn't he?"

"Yes. MP for East Molesworth. I'm sure he'll talk to you if you give him a ring. Very cut up about Jim's death, Terry was."

And in that, at least, Derek Manders was telling the truth.

When Sutcliffe spoke to Stopford in a little room in the Palace of Westminster, he had a decided impression that he was opening old wounds. Stopford was a slightly grey individual, in hair and in personality, but he made it very clear that he spoke (as far as a politician can) from the heart when he said how much he admired Jim Partridge.

"He was almost the only politician I've ever known who was in the game for entirely selfless reasons. There wasn't an ounce of personal push. That's why his career in government never got anywhere. That's why his marriage broke down."

"Yes, I gathered that his wife thought that, without high office, the game wasn't worth the candle."

"Right—that's Penelope all over. Mind you, I said that's why his marriage broke down, but really there were enormous personality differences between them, as Jim found out quite soon after they were married. How she managed to hide her real nature long enough for Jim to propose to her and marry her I can't imagine.

Concealment doesn't come easily to Penny. Her boredom, distaste or contempt are usually all too apparent. Which was a terrible disadvantage in her constituency work."

"You were his confidant over the marriage breakdown?"

"To a degree. To the degree to which Jim was ever likely to confide personal things to anyone. It was a simple case of incompatible personalities and aims. We used to have a lot of heart-to-hearts about it—and then later about the children. We had the last on the evening that he died."

"Did you, now?"

"Yes. In the House of Commons bar. Oh—not putting it away, or anything. Jim wasn't a great drinker. He was talking about his children's upbringing, and about getting them away from their mother as much as possible. He'd become convinced that she was the last person who ought to have the bringing up of young children."

"Was he depressed about this?"

"You mean, was he suicidal? I would have said decidedly no. On the contrary: he was being practical. Trying to find ways of taking over much of their upbringing himself (which would have suited Penelope down to the ground, of course). On the other hand, Jim was *not* an outgoing personality. Even to me—and I knew him as well as any—he kept many private things hidden, or at least veiled. That was why, when I heard of his death, my first thought was to come along to the Yard and say: look, I must have been one of the last people to speak with him, and it *can't* have been suicide. Then, on thinking it over, I thought I couldn't do that, because I didn't really *know*—never really knew—how Jim was thinking."

"When was this last talk?"

"On the evening of the Thursday he died. It was a Dead Thursday—that is, there was very little business, and it petered out early. If he was still in London, and not in Bootham, Thursdays and Fridays were good days for heart-to-hearts. Nobody much around at the House. We parted around ten and he said he was going to walk back to Battersea. It was something I'd often done myself. He took over the flat after me."

"Yes, of course. I knew I'd heard your name before. Tell me, did you talk much, in the last few months, about this Animals' Charter?"

"A fair bit. Naturally."

"I gather he'd been working up to this bill for some time."

"Yes, quite a while. Even while he was still in government he was very distressed about conditions in a factory farm in his constituency. Oh—you know about that?"

"Yes. What did he actually *do* about it—from the beginning?"

"Well, first he tried to lobby various people in relevant ministries to get some action: tighten up regulations, improve inspection procedures, and so on. Nothing doing. Nothing in it for them. By the time he'd finished he'd put a lot of backs up, and no doubt that's why he landed back on the back benches."

"Ah—you think that was the reason?"

"That would be my guess."

"Any particular person responsible?"

Terence Stopford hesitated.

"Well . . . I suppose I owe it to Jim's memory . . .
I think that he'd begun to be convinced, before he died,
that the person who put the PM against him was Evelyn
St John Relph."

"Christ! Who's he, or she?"

"One of the juniors in Agriculture. Tipped for star-
dom, and a very sleazy individual. Personally, I mean,
but Jim became convinced he was sleazy morally as
well."

"Why was that?"

"Relph was one of the key men he talked to, right
from the time he was first worried about factory farming and experiments on animals. He got nowhere with
him—fair words and bugger all otherwise. Jim began
to get reports from this farm he was interested in, and
one of the things he heard was that the place got a tip-
off every time an inspection was in the offing. As he
began voicing his disquiet he got one or two similar
reports from other similar places. He became convinced
that the inspection system had become a farce, because
so many of the establishments always knew in advance.
He was about to put feelers out to people working in
laboratories where experiments on animals took place,
to see if the same were true there."

"Why did he think this Relph character was involved?"

"Initially because his is the responsibility for the inspection of farming premises, and because he has a lush
lifestyle without any known means of supporting it
beyond his ministerial salary, which wouldn't. I think
he got some rather harder evidence after that."

"So you think that as soon as Partridge started meddling in this, Relph got him sacked?"

"That's what Jim thought. Relph has the PM's ear."

"So many people seem to have the Prime Minister's ear."

"It's a much sought-after ear."

It was not an ear, Sutcliffe suspected, that was ever going to incline in his direction. He would have to do without it, which was the easier because he was quite sure that the Prime Minister would be quite unaware of the more dubious goings-on of members of the government: however promiscuous the ear, it would be fed only expurgated versions of the truth. He would have to go about things in his own way—and it was a way made broader and easier by his approaching retirement. If that had not been in the offing, for example, he would never have made his peace with the shade of Jim Partridge by ringing up as he did the Labour MP who had co-sponsored the Animals' Charter.

"Mr Tidmarsh? Sorry to bother you. My name is Sutcliffe. If you remember I spoke to you earlier about James Partridge's death."

"Of course. I remember. Rumour has it you're still burrowing. Getting anywhere?"

"Very slowly, if at all, sir. I gather the Animals' Charter has been dropped?"

" 'Fraid so. Never any chance of getting a bill with any bite in it through the present House. And to be perfectly frank—" (Oh, the frankness of politicians!) —"there was nothing in it for us. Not as a party. Still, it leaves me at a bit of a loose end."

"Ah! Now, what I wanted to know, sir, was whether

Partridge confided to you any suspicions he had about the inspection of intensive farming establishments?"

"Suspicions? I seem to remember once he said these inspections were a bit of a farce—nothing more than that."

"Oh—that's disappointing. Still, I rather imagined he wouldn't . . ."

"Wouldn't? Why wouldn't he?"

"I mean, your being of the opposition party . . ."

Sutcliffe could almost hear the sound of ears being pricked up.

"What? You mean someone in the government? Someone was making sure . . . making sure that all the standards and safeguards were just a farce, like he said."

"You realize I haven't said anything, sir, that would suggest—"

"No, no. Of course not. Your name wouldn't be mentioned. Now, who would it be? Ministry of Agriculture . . . Ministry of Agriculture . . . Of course! That frightful burk Relph! Jim hated his guts, in his quiet way. That's who it would be. Responsible for inspection and standards. There's the making of a real political stink about this. One resignation at the very least. Now, how do I go about nailing him . . ."

Sutcliffe, having reiterated that he himself had said nothing to give Tidmarsh the ideas he seemed to be toying with, rang off, reflecting that policemen all too often had to make use of dubious human material to get a sort of justice done. His dubious material happened to be political. It was now late in the evening, and Sutcliffe had had a hard day: much of it had been spent checking the movements of Antony Craybourne-

Fisk, of Walter Abbot, of Oliver Worthing, and of
Evelyn St John Relph on the evening of December
12th—tiresome, unrewarding work, since he had no
certain knowledge when James Partridge was killed.
On an impulse, before he went home, he took up the
last volume of the London telephone directory and
looked up Snaithe: there it was, entered as "Snaithe,
J. G.," with an address in Claverford Road, Pimlico.
Sutcliffe rang the number.

"Mrs Snaithe? I hope you remember me: we spoke
in a pub in Bootham a few nights ago."

"I thought I knew the voice."

"I just wanted to tell you that I went along to the
meeting, and I enjoyed your piece."

Sue laughed.

"Did you? Funnily enough, quite a lot of people did.
It was very comic, watching them come up and tell
Jerry so afterwards."

"He, then, didn't?"

"He did not, and neither did his WRA Mafia. In
fact, it provoked a fist fight between one of his London
henchmen and one of the locals, but I gather the situation was so tense that it only needed a spark to set
it off."

"What did your husband actually say afterwards?"

"Well, it was rather difficult for him to say much.
After all those protestations about my independence.
Finally he said that he'd always maintained that my
views were my own, of *course* they were, absolutely
my own affair, but did I have to broadcast such *con-
troversial* opinions in so public a manner? Controver-
sial! As if he hasn't always loved controversy! I said he

should have made it clear that as his wife I was in a
position rather like the Queen's: I could have what
opinions I liked provided I kept them entirely to myself. We had rather a jolly row. It doesn't matter greatly
now . . ."

"Oh?"

"I'm leaving him as soon as it's decent after the election. Do you think I ought to stay with him longer if
he wins, or if he loses? Anyway, apart from the fact
of not *liking* him any more—just finding him rather
exciting now and then—this business really crystallized
my feelings about the hypocrisy of the man. I really
couldn't go on living with such a two-faced bastard. It
made me wonder—"

"Yes?"

"How Mrs Pecksniff felt, all the time she was living
with Seth."

16

Declaration

On the morning of February 27th—a dismal, dank morning it started—the polling booths opened promptly at seven o'clock, and for the next hour or two the electoral officials sat around staring at the walls, as a mere trickle of voters came in on their way to work, or, more frequently, to get early to the Job Centres or the Social Security offices. By nine, however, the loud-hailers of all three main parties were out urging people to vote, and the thin trickle was swelling to a stream.

By ten the candidates were busy, out around the town, being cheery or hortatory; but in reality this was not their day, or not their day until counting actually started. More important were the people with cars whom all the main parties sent out to ferry to the polls any of their voters who might have difficulty getting there. The Conservatives could call on a whole fleet of rather splendid cars, but the owners thereof were otherwise occupied or reluctant to act as chauffeurs, so the cars

were driven very often by young helpers from elsewhere, who drove the voters a merry dance around
Bootham's maze of no-thoroughfares and one-way streets
("Come along, young man, it's my morning coffee-
time!") and put hundreds of pounds into the local garage owners' pockets after minor traffic accidents. The
Labour Party solved this, in their fleet of less grand
cars, by having a local driver paired with a London
helper who would fetch from their houses the ailing or
crippled voters. This apparently worked better, but the
bitter silence between the two in the front seats was all
too obvious to those sitting in the back, and the London
helpers' cheery cries of "Come on, Ma" to elderly ladies
caused at least five of them, in the secrecy of the polling
booth, to put their crosses against the Social Democratic candidate, with villainous expressions on their
faces. The Social Democrats ran a much more rackety
taxi service, partly because their organization was mere
middle-class improvisation. Voters were ringing up, aggrieved, right up to ten o'clock in the evening, inquiring
for transport that had been promised them; and one
old gentleman set out, despairing, for the polling station
at a quarter to ten, being picked up exhausted in a
doorway by a friendly policeman at ten past, saying he
hadn't missed voting in an election since the khaki election of 1918, and by gum! he hadn't missed this one
either.

Voting suited Bootham. In the main square Yelping
Lord Crotch had teamed up with the John Lennon
Lives candidate and a group of supporting musicians,
and they were creating quite a carnival atmosphere in
the dank February chill; and in another corner of the

square, on a dais, the Transcendental Meditation candidate was meditating transcendentally. Sutcliffe observed them both when he arrived back in Bootham
around lunch-time. By then there were thick knots of
voters converging on the Old Grammar School, the
most central polling station in the town, and outside
the school's gates he saw scattered media men waiting
to interview voters when they came out. Being the centre
of attention suited that sense of self-importance which
is a Yorkshireman's birthright, and several people even
buttonholed television reporters to explain to them in
depth their reasons for not voting at all.

The declaration of poll was expected about midnight,
and, popping his head into one of the central hotels,
Sutcliffe found that several of the media persons intended driving south as soon as their stories were filed,
apparently their way of showing their opinion of
Bootham. He therefore managed to engage a room for
the night, though still at a quite exorbitant rate. He
spent the rest of the day sampling the sights and sounds
and smells of the by-election, and glimpsed all the main
candidates at one time or another, in loud-speaker vans,
or hail-fellowing in the streets: Antony Craybourne-
Fisk was being driven around by Walter Abbot, which
could not have done him much good in most people's
eyes; Oliver Worthing was wandering distractedly in
the vicinity of the Town Hall, having lost his entourage;
Jerry Snaithe was being driven around on the back of
a lorry, exuberant, shouting slogans, but somehow
managing to resemble some aspirant Führer, still in the
preliminary, beer-cellar-putsch phase of his career.

It was quite by chance, later, that Sutcliffe came upon

Jerry again, just as polling ended. Jerry had kept it up all day: personal appearance at a polling station here, impromptu speech there, driven here there and everywhere by one or other of his "team," and talking most of the time. The end of polling was bound to be a bit of a let-down for Jerry, the time when his fix began to wear off. Normally he wasn't a great fraternizer, unless there was something to be gained from it. Others went off from meetings to a pub, but Jerry went off on his own to plan the next meeting. Now, however, in the last minutes of polling and before going to the Town Hall with the other candidates for the count, Jerry let himself be pulled into a pub by a little group of his London young men. Several of these were teetotal, refusing above all to drink beer, on account of the fortunes that flowed into Tory Party funds from the major breweries. Some, however, had managed to square it with their principles to drink Real Ale, and it was that that Sutcliffe found them supping when, having observed their progress from Labour Party Headquarters to the Ironmaster's Arms, he followed them in at a discreet distance and bought himself a pint of the normal commercial brew. He stood by the bar for a moment and watched the group: in among them was Jerry's pet Machiavel whom he had met before, and he was raising his mug in a toast: "All power to the workers! To the great swing to the Left!" They all let out a good-humoured roar at this, but Jerry was responding with his mouth; he was not responding with his eyes.

For Jerry—and this explains what was to follow—was an experienced political animal who, still better than Oliver Worthing, could read signs and do calculations. And, whatever the more naive expectations of his henchmen might be, Jerry did not believe that he had won. Nothing, of course, was certain with the blessed British electoral system, and the blessed British voter, but Jerry was pretty sure that he had not made it. So, in fact, was Fred Long, Jerry's electoral agent. There had been enough Labour supporters who had said they would not be voting for him—because he was too left-wing, because he was not a solid Union man, because he was an interloper from London, however much he might think to fool them by putting on a fancy Yorkshire voice—to convince them both that he could not have made it to the top of the poll. For a left-wing candidate will always find it hard to bring over significant numbers of floating voters, and if he has alienated some part of his own people, that was what he imperatively would have to do. It was a bitter pill for Jerry, but he now realized that tomorrow morning he would be just one more member of the doomed Greater London Council—no more, no less.

It was partly the bitterness of this feeling, partly the vacuum at the heart of his emotional being as his fix ended, partly his flair for the theatrical, his kamikaze instinct, that moulded his response when Sutcliffe came over to the red-rosetted little group.

"Mr Snaithe? I don't want to spoil your party, but my name is Sutcliffe. You may have heard I'm looking into James Partridge's death. You're the only one of the major candidates I haven't had a word with so far, but I wonder if some time I might? If you can't manage tomorrow, perhaps I could ring you up and arrange a time when you get back to London?"

A graveyard hush had fallen over the group. The Enemy was at hand, was within the walls.

"Good Lord," said Jerry, looking at him as if he were some kind of insect, yet with an element of calculation in his eye. "It's the fuzz, boys! How bloody bizarre! What on earth can you want with me? I never knew Jim Partridge, you know. I'm one of the bogeyman figures for people like that."

"I realize that, sir. It's purely a matter of routine."

"Then why," said Jerry, draining his glass, "not make it the present?" He looked meaningfully at his infant Mafia. "If there's going to be victimization, let's make it as public as possible. I suppose you want me to step along to the station?"

And he walked Sutcliffe out of the pub, rather than vice-versa, leaving his little squad of henchmen to feed sensational stories to the media that would make him the hero of left-wing myth-making for many months to come. It was, Sutcliffe decided, a wonderful display of confidence. Electoral humiliation would be forgotten, and only memories of police victimization would remain.

The police station was two minutes away. Mostly they walked in silence, Jerry striding it out, with a tiny, almost schoolboyish smile playing on the corners of his mouth. The only time he spoke he said:

"This is pure totalitarianism."

(Jerry was an expert on totalitarianism. He had been loud in condemnation of it in El Salvador, the Philippines and South Africa, loud in praise of it in Cuba, Ethiopia and the Soviet Union. You could say he had an open mind on the subject.)

"I don't think they generally give you the choice of when you are to be taken in, in totalitarian countries," said Sutcliffe.

At the station, most of the policemen on duty were out on the streets, or at the Town Hall for the count and declaration, when things could sometimes get rough. There was a sergeant on the desk, of course, and he took one look at Sutcliffe's companion and responded to his polite request for a room by showing him to a superintendent's office. Sutcliffe had become quietly familiar to the Bootham police, and Jerry, over the last few weeks, had become as well known in Bootham as second-rank royalty, or the people who do pet-food commercials on television.

"Basically you're quite right, sir," said Sutcliffe, as they settled in comfortably with a cup of machine-coffee in front of them. "There isn't any particular reason why I should interview you. Though of course I wouldn't want you to feel left out, either."

Jerry was tensed up, and Sutcliffe was conscious, as he had never been when seeing him on his campaign, of the physical rather than the political animal—strong, in peak condition, trained. He was entering the interview like a crack marksman preparing for a duel.

"Most amusing," Jerry said, stretching his mouth.

"So far a lot of my time has been spent looking at Mr Partridge's parliamentary work, and I've been specially interested in this so-called Animals' Charter. There were a lot of what you might call special interests involved there."

"Too bloody right. A real little nest of them," said Jerry, stirring his coffee with his large, strong hands.

"I heard you'd been around to that Fascist bastard Walter Abbot. I notice nothing has come of it, though."

"We have to be careful, sir. You in the House of Commons—should you be elected—can say pretty much anything you like about anybody, and be protected by privilege. We have to be sure we have a case before we say anything at all. That's a particular problem as far as the death of James Partridge is concerned: we're not even sure it *is* a case of murder."

"Quite," said Jerry Snaithe.

"It was natural to take a look at the man's political opponents, as well as the people he antagonized in his own party. After all, politics has become a pretty violent game in the last ten or fifteen years, and the violence can spill over on to anyone, however uncontroversial. A reporter gave me a tip that the election I ought to be looking at was the last one—the one at which Mr Worthing was also standing."

"Oh yes, those rumours," said Jerry casually, stretching out his legs rather in the manner of Derek Manders, and quite as irritatingly. "I don't think there was anything in them. Anyway, I believe in fighting on the issues."

"I'm sure you do. Only in one respect what the reporter said was wrong: he said that you and Mr Craybourne-Fisk and the rest were Johnny-come-latelies who had only been adopted as candidates since the death of Partridge. Now that, I realize now, is one of those things that may be classed as true in fact but misleading in implication."

"Oh? I don't see that. It certainly is true in fact as far as I'm concerned. I was adopted on January the fourteenth."

"Quite, sir. But your nomination was virtually certain from the moment your group—the WRA isn't it called? So confusing all these initials—got control of the Bootham party. One of your young helpers told me that—a very helpful, friendly young man."

"He was speaking out of turn. It's nonsense."

"Well, I've checked up with local Labour stalwarts, and they all agree that the WRA had things sewn up in the constituency party by November."

"So what?"

"It's a motive, sir. You were sure of the nomination, if you wanted it, but there would have been no poll before the General Election, which is anything up to two years away. Only by Jim Partridge's death was there a chance of your being MP for Bootham before that."

Jerry Snaithe stretched his mouth again.

"It's pretty bloody flimsy."

"Not to someone in my line of work. I assure you, I've seen murder done for very much less than a parliamentary seat. Or, rather, the chance to fight for a parliamentary seat. Particularly as in your case there was an added spur."

"What was that?"

"The abolition of the Greater London Council. In a matter of months, or so it seems, it will have disappeared, and so will your platform. The best you can hope for is a seat on one of the London local councils, which is all that will be left. There won't be much national or media interest in *them*. In my experience, sir, politicians usually have something of the performer in them. They like an audience, reviews. Going from the GLC to the Pimlico District Council would be like going from the West End to one of those little pub theatres. And then, all at once, there came the chance to get into the National Theatre . . ."

Jerry smiled, this time a genuine smile. He was beginning to enjoy himself. He was, indeed, shaping up to give a performance.

"Well, well: you really seem to have adopted the media view of politicians, Superintendent. Shall I allow you motive? Right. I had a motive—along with many others."

"Quite. Along with many others. But Mr Craybourne-Fisk didn't have *that* motive: his selection was highly uncertain, and he'd never been heard of in this constituency before James Partridge's death. And, for all my digging, I never found the shadow of another motive for him, not for murdering James Partridge. Into all sorts of murky financial skulduggery—with Mrs Partridge, Derek Manders, and dreaming up something with Walter Abbot, should he become the MP here—all that, yes. But I couldn't make any connection between his financial skulduggery and the murder of James Partridge."

"So you blithely forget about it?"

"I am about to retire from the CID, sir. I have a restricted brief. No doubt before very long he'll sail so close to the wind that his boat overturns. It's not, I suspect, a very good boat. Well, now, I grant you there are others with motive around, and a motive doesn't actually get us very far. So we come to opportunity. Here we have great problems, because we don't really know the time he died. So that Walter Abbot, arriving home from a meeting of European farmers in an organization called EuroAg—I fancy you

and I might agree about *them*, sir—got into Heathrow
from Strasbourg at ten o'clock and spent the night in
a Kensington hotel. Penelope Partridge was apparently
home all evening, Craybourne-Fisk had a meeting that
ended before ten, Oliver Worthing had a college meeting, but I gather it was an early evening one, and it
was over by eight. He could have been in his car, down
the M1, and been on the Vauxhall Bridge well before
midnight."

"And I? What was I doing? I haven't the remotest
recollection."

"You, sir, were at a meeting of the Leisure Activities
Committee, as I gather you frequently are on Thursdays. Now this interested me. Your wife tells me you
are not a fraternizer after meetings. Your meeting that
night ended about nine-forty—as they often do, or
around that time. Jim Partridge finished a conversation
with an MP friend at the Commons about ten—also a
common occurrence on a Thursday. Now, if we set
you walking along the left bank of the river towards
Battersea, and Jim Partridge along the right bank of the
river towards Pimlico—you the faster walker, I would
guess, sir, a strider, if ever I saw one . . . then you
might well cross the Vauxhall Bridge towards Pimlico,
and he cross it towards Battersea, let's say about half
past ten. Which is when the night-watchman in the
office block heard a cry, and went to have a look over
the river."

"Oh? Who was that? I hadn't heard about him."

"Just a solitary chap, soaking up cans of lager to
while away the long winter evening."

"Not a very reliable witness, then, I would have
thought, Superintendent."

"Not reliable at all, sir. I can imagine a defence law-yer making mincemeat of him if we ever put him up in court. The trouble is, though, that I've always placed a fair bit of trust in that report, because after all that *was* about where he'd be on his way home, and if, say, Abbot or Worthing had killed him on the bridge much later, what was he doing there? How had they got him out of his flat and over to that spot? No, I've always fancied ten-thirty as the time of the killing. And you, sir, could well have been there. And, what's more, been there before."

"Before?"

"I mean that there could have been previous occa-sions on that bridge when you could have been coming home from your Thursday meetings, and Partridge could have been coming back on a Dead Thursday from the House of Commons, and you could have passed. Per-haps if you realized that this was *his* bridge, the one he always crossed the river on, you yourself might have chosen that one, rather than, say, Westminster, and chosen to walk home rather than take a bus or tube. In case you had the chance of seeing the sitting MP for the seat that you were conspiring—"

"Loaded word, Superintendent."

"Manœuvring?"

"Still loaded."

"—working to get the Labour nomination for your-self. Now, don't say you wouldn't have recognized him, sir. You're a political animal, he had been a junior minister. You would have made it your business to know the sitting member for Bootham. You may have been unknown to him, but he can't have been to you.

And if your paths had crossed on the bridge once, twice, or more often before, one can imagine a little idea, a possibility, sporting around in the back areas of your mind."

"Right. I get your drift, Superintendent. It's possible, I grant you that—though I think that ordinary minds would find it a touch fantastic."

Jerry Snaithe's accent, as he sparred with Sutcliffe, had taken on a sort of drawl—really, in fact, an upper-class drawl.

"I'm inclined to agree with you, sir. In fact, there is much about politics that the ordinary mind finds a trifle fantastic."

"What comes next? What about the means? How did I, do you think, kill him?"

"Ah, well, there I had a tiny idea from the moment I saw the pathologist's reports. I've had a fair bit to do with deaths, in the course of my police career. Now I'm retiring I hope to have much less, while preparing for my own. When I heard about those dull bruises on the left-hand face and temple—bruises that could have been caused by contact with a boat, or the supporting pillars of the bridge, but which the doctor was somehow rather dubious about—I remembered the body of a man who'd been killed in a brawl in the back yard of a pub. He'd been killed by one of the killer karate blows that leave practically no trace—a blow with the open hand against the side of the face and temple. Fortunately in this case there were witnesses, and no question as to who had done it. Actually, sir, he was an ex-SAS man like yourself: received his karate training in the Service."

Jeremy Snaithe shifted in his chair, but looked at Sutcliffe hard and long.

"My army service is a matter of record. I've never tried to hide it."

"Certainly it's a matter of record. But you've never actually proclaimed it, have you, sir? It would hardly go down well with most of your supporters."

"It was a youthful aberration, a hangover from public school. Thank God I grew out of that phase."

"But did you actually grow out of that phase, sir? My information is that you left the SAS, very reluctantly, under a cloud. What was the story, now? Three rather pathetic Palestinian terrorists, obviously incompetent, holding a hostage in the Israeli consulate in Liverpool, back in 1974. The police were expecting to be able to talk them out without much difficulty, but the SAS were there in reserve, as usual, and you went in through a back door, on your own initiative, and the result was one dead terrorist, two severely injured, and a hostage with a bullet through his thigh. It was shortly after that, by mutual agreement, that you parted company with the Service. When you first went into Labour politics you swung, as people like you so often do, from one extreme to the other—one set of whites becomes black, another set of blacks becomes white. You have to have absolutes to believe in totally. What certainly didn't alter was the fact that you had the training of a killer."

"Which you think I used on Jim Partridge?"

"Which I think you used on Jim Partridge. Let's put the most charitable interpretation possible on it: which I think, completely on impulse, finding that bridge unusually empty of traffic, you used on Jim Partridge."

There was silence in the interview room. Jerry Snaithe continued looking hard at Sutcliffe. Then suddenly, quite unexpectedly, he smiled.

"Prove it," he said.

Oh, that smile! How often had Sutcliffe seen it in the course of this investigation. From Arthur Tidmarsh, from Antony Craybourne-Fisk, from Derek Manders. It was the smile of engaging political roguery. It was the smile that said: Look—you know, I know, that I'm in it for what I can get out of it, but—what the hell—aren't there rogues in your profession too? It was a smile that mixed complicity with a dare, a smile that invited you into the circle of clever rogues, a smile that presupposed a camaraderie of the self-seeking and the morally suspect. It was a smile that told Sutcliffe that his long-shot guess had been right.

"Oh, there's really no question of that, sir," he said, easily and amicably, and as he said it he got up.

"Oh?" said Jerry, looking up at him almost aggrieved, as if he had a sense of anti-climax, as if a duel he was going to participate in had been called off.

"No question at all. I've known that pretty much all along, sir. That's why I've done much of this in my own time. Once the boys doing the leg-work had established in the first day or two after the murder that nobody had actually seen anything suspicious, and taking that in conjunction with the state of the body, which presented no indisputable signs of murder, I knew this meant there was hardly the remotest chance of getting a conviction. After motive, opportunity, means, there comes that vital question of evidence. Anything I've done in this case, sir, has really been for my own satisfaction."

"An abstract passion for justice?" inquired Jerry, sardonically.

"An abstract passion for *truth*, sir. I'm afraid there is little chance of justice. You will go back to your political career, whatever it may be, I'll go into retirement. You will know, I will know, and perhaps one or two others will suspect. But justice? No, alas—because I believe in justice—you'll never be brought to book."

"And you're just letting me go now?" Jerry asked, with that aggrieved bewilderment.

"That's right, sir. What else can I do? Are you thinking it would make a better story if I kept you here all through the count and the declaration? Make you more of a victim-hero to your friends and supporters, after you've lost? I'm sure your young henchmen have prepared the ground. No, sir, you're free to go. It's only five past eleven, and three minutes to the Town Hall. You'll probably have an hour before the declaration. I don't have to throw you out of the station, do I, sir?"

With another smile of complicity, which somehow came out slightly cracked, Jerry got up and marched out of the room with that long, striding, military walk, that Tory country landowner's walk, that suddenly made Sutcliffe think that in a way, James Partridge had been killed by one of his own party.

When Sutcliffe had gathered up his papers, he went out to the front office and found the duty sergeant looking intently at a portable television set placed unorthodoxly on his counter.

"Seems like we're famous, sir. Fancy a cup of cold

tea?" And he looked hard at Superintendent Sutcliffe with a policeman's version of that smile of complicity.

"Thanks. I often find cold tea warming on a night like this." And so, gratefully, it proved. "What have they been saying?" he asked, nodding at the set, with its chaotic pictures of piles of ballot papers and distraught officials.

"Speculating about this Snaithe's absence from the count, first of all. Then they got this rumour that he was at the station here. That gave the commentators a chance to talk about rumours concerning James Partridge's death that they said had been surfacing now and then in the course of the campaign."

"Hmmm. Jerry's little helpers have been busy."

"Why would they do that, sir?"

"At a nod from their boss. I think he knows he's lost the election and he aims to divert attention by some sort of sensation about police victimization. It will go down very well with all the people who support him, except that I let him go so soon everyone will know we hardly had time to do more than pass the time of day. Anyway, it's a new source of excitement for him, it will satisfy the craving for a bit. But when I let him go, you could feel the disappointment: he was banking on an all-night grilling, and inch-high headlines."

"What's behind it, sir? Is it the death of Mr Partridge, like they've been saying?"

"Oh yes, it's the death of Partridge. The murder of Partridge. Only it's never going to be that officially now."

And sitting there over their "cold tea," and then over another, Sutcliffe told the sergeant something of his poking round into the death of Bootham's MP. He was just getting round to Jerry, his SAS training, and his opportunity, when the gentleman-commentator at Bootham Town Hall began to show signs of excitement.

"It's coming . . . I think the Declaration is imminent . . . yes, the Returning Officer is coming forward . . ."

Sutcliffe broke off as a heavy and self-important individual laboriously unburdened himself of the customary phrases:

"As returning officer for the constituency of Bootham East . . ."

"Get on with it," muttered Sutcliffe.

". . . the following votes cast: Edward Armstrong, the Bring Back Hanging candidate, two hundred and fifty . . ."

"Oh Christ, we've got to go through the loonies," swore Sutcliffe, to the offence of the sergeant, who had voted for Armstrong himself.

"Booth, Helen, Women for the Bomb, one hundred and six; Carter, Edward, National Front, six hundred and twenty; Craybourne-Fisk, Antony, twelve thousand, three hundred and sixteen . . ."

The Town Hall was rent by cheers, but Sutcliffe's sharp ear detected a hollowness behind them, an element of whistling in the dark, as if Antony's supporters knew that was not good enough.

"If I'm not mistaken, Bootham has not elected one of the New Tories," he murmured.

"Crotch, Peter Thomas, Top of the Pops," pursued the official, impervious to any sense of the ridiculous, "seven hundred and twenty; Fermor-Meddibrook, Constance, Home Rule for England, one hundred and seven; Fust, Jason, John Lennon Lives, forty-seven; Manciple, Michael, Richard III Was Innocent, seventeen; Nubble, Frederick, Communist, five hundred and ninety-four; Popperwell, June, Britain Out of the Common Market, one thousand and ten . . ."

"A surprisingly good result there," purred the commentator.

"Get on, you burk," snarled Sutcliffe.

"Singh, Percival Richard, Transcendental Meditation, eighty-six; Snaithe, Jeremy, Labour Party, thirteen thousand and forty-seven . . ."

Again, tremendous cheers rent the Town Hall, but again . . . could it be . . . ?

"Ward, Humphrey, Transvestite Meditation, seven; Worthing, Oliver, Social Democratic Party, fourteen thousand one hundred and—"

But his voice was drowned by a tremendous yell of middle-class radicals, countered by howls of disappointment from the young supporters of Jerry, and in the body of the hall the cameras focused on the beginnings of several scuffles, with the police immediately moving in. If the vote for Zachariah Zzugg, the I'm Coming Last candidate, ever got announced, Sutcliffe did not hear it.

"Well, well, well," he said. "I wondered if he'd make it."

"Can't understand it, myself," said the sergeant. "Seems a funny result for Bootham."

"I don't know about that. It's vindicated the democratic process: it's sent to Westminster someone no-

body much wanted, but nobody much objected to, and
seen packing two people whom little groups of enthu-
siasts liked, but people in general couldn't stand. It
means that people saw through them."

"Tell me more about this Snaithe, sir . . ."

And Sutcliffe did, breaking off only when, on the
tiny screen, he saw the defeated candidates coming forward to give their speeches, their verbal gestures of
acquiescence to the democratic will. Antony was first
of the major ones, hideously disappointed behind an
upper lip that was not so much stiff as paralysed.

". . . Perhaps I shouldn't have hoped that at this
time, after the government has had to take tough
decisions—necessary, right decisions, but tough ones
for the people of Bootham—that I could maintain a
majority won by a very much loved predecessor . . ."

"Bullshit," said Sutcliffe.

Jeremy hid his disappointment better. Was not his
speciality coming up for the fourth time?

"We've seen during this by-election a media campaign of vilification and misrepresentation of unprec-
edented proportions, culminating tonight in events that
I think most of you will have heard about by now.
When the working people of this country are fed a diet
of lies of this kind, we shouldn't be surprised . . ."

"Bullshit," said Sutcliffe, and in a moment turned
away from the box, on which Oliver Worthing was
now meandering through a speech of thanks both too
long and too grammatically convoluted.

"What you're saying, sir," pursued the sergeant, "is
that you think he did it, that Labour bloke."

"I know he did it. He gave me that smile, that smile

that said: 'OK, I admit it, but prove it. You never will.'
And he was quite right. I never will."

"Is there *no* way, sir? Surely it's early days yet?"

"No way, except by an actual, unimpeachable witness, or preferably more than one. It's not early days for witnesses. The time's long past for them."

"What you're saying, then, sir, is that he's going to get away with murder?"

Sutcliffe downed the last of his cold tea.

"Don't politicians always?"

17

Inquests

By-elections resemble bodies that have died unnaturally: inevitably they have inquests that sit upon them.

The political hacks had their say in the later editions the next day, or in the Friday weeklies and the Sunday heavies. They fed the votes, the swings, the turnout into the mincing machine of their psephologically-attuned minds, and came up with the conclusion that it was a triumph for the Social Democrats and a humiliation for the government. Then they went back to El Vino's to forget about it all.

The Social Democrats' inquest was really more of a small-scale orgy. The whole parliamentary party, all seven of them, were gathered in the party's London headquarters, and when the result was announced they filled the available floor space with a rapturous dance. Since all seven members of the parliamentary party were male, it was fortunate that the police's interest in MPs' sexual habits was confined to sending their prettier PCs

216

into the gay clubs of Soho to seduce them, and that they had not yet woken up to what could go on in party headquarters. The next day, when Oliver Worthing came to London, he found to his surprise that he had already been made his party's spokesman on education.

The Labour leader sat at home watching on television, knowing that he would be telephoned for a comment as soon as the results were known. His feelings when the Labour candidate was a left-wing trouble-maker who had wangled himself the candidacy by thoroughly conspiratorial means were always ambiguous, and when he heard through a phone call from the Labour Agent that Jerry Snaithe was being interviewed by the police in connection with the murder of James Partridge, he became very het-up and Welsh indeed.

"Thank God we lost" was his reaction when the result was announced, though when one of the national newspapers rang him minutes later, he had a very different rigmarole at his practised fingertips.

But the final, authoritative judgment on the by-election was pronounced from No. 10, Downing Street.

It was one of those not-too-busy Fridays when the absence of important business in the House meant that time could be given to a consideration, not of day-to-day, bread-and-butter matters, but of more visionary schemes. Thus, while lackeys were scurrying hither and thither leaking libellous titbits of information to account for the poor showing of the Conservative candidate, the Prime Minister was sat at a desk stewing over a draft speech advocating the

abolition of the old age pension. A knotty passage in
the argument had just been reached when the phone
rang.

"Yes? . . . The Chairman? Put him on at once . . .
Well, that *was* a poor showing at Bootham yesterday."

From the end of the line came a high-pitched, fluttery
voice.

"I quite agree, Prime Minister, but—"

"A poor candidate, *I* would have said. A quite un-
suitable candidate for *that* constituency."

"I'm glad you realize—"

"If you'll just let me finish, John. You people at
Central Office should have given better advice to the
selectors. And I don't understand why the election had
to be *hurried* in the way it was: it gave the impression
that we wanted to get it out of the way before the
Budget—"

"But, Prime Minister, *you*—"

"No excuses. There are going to have to be a lot of
socks pulled up at Central Office, and I'll expect you
to see that they are."

The phone was put firmly and finally down. On the
blank wall in the office, on which were invisibly written
the names of all the cabinet and all the party officials,
there appeared against that of the party chairman one
more black mark.

Then the Prime Minister returned to the text of the
speech:

"Surely it is vital to encourage enterprise and initiative in the old—*especially* in the old . . ."

It was Business As Usual.